NEGATIVE SPACE

NEGATIVE SPACE

Robert Steiner

COUNTERPOINT | BERKELEY

Library of Congress Cataloging-in-Publication Data

Steiner, Robert, 1948–
Negative space / by Robert Steiner.
p. cm.
ISBN 978-1-58243-642-5
1. Married people—Fiction. 2. Loss (Psychology)—Fiction.
3. Domestic fiction. I. Title.

PS3569.T376N44 2010
813'.54—dc22

2010017801

Cover design by Ann Weinstock
Interior design by Neuwirth & Associates, Inc.

Printed in the United States of America

COUNTERPOINT
1919 Fifth Street
Berkeley, CA 94710

www.counterpointpress.com

Distributed by Publishers Group West

10 9 8 7 6 5 4 3 2 1

NEGATIVE SPACE

I n the hour before sunrise, I lie beside the woman I love, studying her face in the darkness, as if I have studied it in a dream, just as I used to awaken in the night, covering her body with mine because in a dream my body covered hers. I know she is unfaithful to me because I dream of it, so in the darkness I see in her sleeping face the need to be elsewhere, to be someone else elsewhere, with someone who is not me. I observe the face of her infidelity, resting my head beside hers, my eyes watching hers in case they open. I slip from our bed to an armchair while my wife wrestles the dawn—ash yellow, or ash gray, now and again red as a peach. While my wife is unfaithful to me, she is faithful to her new needs, among which her lover is the most urgent. During the hour before sunrise, in the torpor of my wife's infidelity, I smoke in an armchair in the bedroom because everything has changed, and nothing will be the same, and what I have believed between nothing and everything is no longer what it was, whatever it was. I begin to discern day from night, then true from untrue, then her torpor from my despair, then I think *I am*, our shortest sentence, the simplest observation to thwart death.

For those who have found debasement through love, reminding them that they will die alone and ruined, the voice of infidelity is the most erotic they will hear. A familiar voice recites an impossible story of sexual betrayal, an intimate voice suddenly as distant as the thousands of years of confessions that have destroyed hundreds of millions of lives. This is as close to meaning as life gets, I thought, when the voice of the woman I love, whose body I know inch upon inch, admitted she had kissed the lips and genitals of a sexual stranger, exchanging intimacy with me for intimacy with him, who now knows my wife's body inch upon inch. She whispered to me because the air was silent at the end of siesta, the warmest hour of our day, but her confession was no less bold for being unspeakable. She whispered in curves, in waves and troughs, of the imperfection of human beings, of humans imperfectly in love, to which I replied, at any opportunity, that love was not perfect the way her breasts were perfect, or the wine perfect, or sunset over the sea, and not perfect like the caramel volutes of her exposed labia. As the woman I love confessed on our terrace overlooking an olive grove three hundred years old, we watched the sun swoon. There was a bottle of Beaune Margaux, and a hard Camargue cheese on our terrace during the confession, as there would be a box of filterless Gitanes, wood matches as long as bird legs snapping in the dark, olives from the olive grove, bats against the sky. I heard my wife uncork the Beaune Margaux we had found in the rain in Beaune, the day she first lied about her adultery. As she arrived on the terrace, the confession began to be a confession when I saw, out of the corner of my eye, that she was looking at me out of the corner of her eye. When my wife of twenty years presented wine and a ski slope of cheese in the pouch of our raffia basket, I told her that the taste of her thigh was still on my tongue, a memory I invented for the moment. As she leaned across the chaise to fill my glass, the incidental curve of one breast evoked the jealousy I had been shaping over the weeks I waited for her to confess. I wanted to hear how her desire had created my jealousy, so as soon as I invented the memory of tasting her thigh in the hot sun on the previous day, I tasted it—salty, sandy, moist with sweat. Before stepping onto the terrace, my wife tuned the radio beyond the dark news of the universe (it is dying) to the muted trumpet of a dead trumpeter, either to remind herself of a reality beyond infidelity, or to argue that one did not exist. *Remember what you suspected when I returned from Paris?* she asked, leaning across me with the Beaune Margaux. *It's true,* she said, filling both our glasses.

On our terrace, overlooking the olive grove at sunset, my wife looked like someone being looked at, someone conscious of being born to be looked at like an object, the way certain red figure vases in certain museums look looked at. Her *otherness* I had accepted, as everyone lives with the truth that the person to whom they are closest in the world is different from them and, because of it, capable of anything. Confessing her betrayal, my wife looked as if she felt *other* to herself, not only to me, as if she had taken a blow to the head, a concussion that left her with a tenuous grasp of the familiar world, as if it were crumbling between her fingers. Perhaps she felt disembodied because, by giving voice to her infidelity, the burden transformed betrayal into something weightier than the known world, something that she knew would devastate the man she had loved for decades, loved until the moment she loved someone else instead. Since my wife was holding the wine against her cheek as the confession began, her glass filled with sunset, so years later sunset would remind me of my wife's infidelity. Sunset betrays the day, I would think, watching sunset months later, but it was no less beautiful for its crime against humanity. Her lips were white and dry, so I motioned the woman I love to sip the wine and, though she did, she sipped very little, like someone afraid of being sick. The more merciless her confession, the more human she became, though she had never been inhuman to me, at least not since she had been the object of all my desires twenty years before, an object of lust as well as of mystery. Twenty years later, my jealousy objectified the woman I love again, reminding me that she had been the object of my passion before she was the woman I love or my wife, let alone the object of someone else's passion and the woman I love who was about to leave. Listening to her begin her confession, I recalled that I had needed absolute possession of her when we first met, before I loved her, and that loving her had made a hostile universe liveable. Now that her lover desired possession of her, and she of him, as she had of me, I was the undesirable in the universe. On the terrace, overlooking the three-hundred-year-old olive grove, above cobbled Moorish streets that ring of footfalls in the darkness, my wife recited the secret erotic life she had been leading, during which I had raised suspicions daily, sometimes more often. It had taken months before she realized what her adulterous life had become, and only as a result of living each day unfaithfully was she prepared to hear herself tell me the truth. *If you had kept your suspicions to yourself,* my wife said, *I could have understood everything sooner, but your accusations prolonged the suffering for both of us,* for all of us, she corrected.

Staring into her wine as if she had found a fly in it, my wife said that by the time the wanton acts she committed had become demonstrations of love, lying to me was inevitable, despite knowing that the deceit would be more painful than learning of her secret erotic life. She accused me of driving her into someone else's arms, or if not, then yearning for it, which seemed to her more perverse than the perverse acts she enjoyed, and continued to enjoy, with her lover. I might as well have apologized, as if my suspicions were worse than her affair, not only insulting but also comprising *my* secret erotic life. She accused me of bad faith, *mauvaise foi* she said, finding her voice in two languages, a *mauvaise foi*, which, she insisted, might have encouraged her infidelity the way learning your loved one loves pornography can lead to pornographic acts with someone other than your loved one. She recoiled when I touched her bare knee because she wanted to punish me for my suspicions, or because they had been correct, or because my touch reminded her of the lover's touch, or because my touch distracted her from the confession she intended to recite before freeing herself of the shame my touch evoked. My wife had committed adultery, without admitting it, until she had fallen in love, when it was no longer an adulterous affair but the dramatic manner in which she met the love of her life, giving her unbridled power that even my jealousy could not address. When she said she loved someone else, her words swept me away, as if I were seeing her for the first time across a room, or as if she were confessing that she had fallen in love with me. Because the woman I love had found a different voice at sunset on our terrace, she renewed my passion for her, and because another man had touched her body, I wanted to touch it, too. In the distance, the olive grower stepped from his doorway for a glance at the grove, clearing his throat to remind me that from their bedroom window, if it was open, he would be able to hear our conversation, assuming we raised our voices. To his right, a pale light flickered against a shutter of the window—his wife on her way to bed, looking, in her snood and nightgown, like a wife by Vermeer.

When I told the woman I love that I expected her to answer my most invasive questions, she replied that, while she empathized, I had no right to violate the privacy she and her lover shared. I thought I must have misheard, or that my wife forgot she had violated *our* privacy in order to begin a new one elsewhere. She apologized when I reminded her, saying that she should not have said it the way she said it, not so much to spare my feelings but to spare us both the risk of bombs exploding before she had an opportunity to explain her suffering, as well as why, where, and with whom she had been suffering it. *I don't want bombs,* she said, *not until I tell you what I have to tell you.* My wife assured me that she had said nothing to her lover concerning me or the intimacies of our life together, and, but for the adultery, she had respected our marriage. Both of us, I should say each of us, paused to sip the Beaune Margaux, adding a Gitanes to the menu. Below, olive trees against the leaking sun rose toward our terrace, an approaching army of tall thin warriors about to chuck spears. I said, *I'm speechless* to the darkness in front of me, having heard what I would have considered an impossible sentence in my wife's voice, but what was only the first of many impossible sentences, or why it is called confession. My wife said, into the rim of her wineglass, that she had not admitted the existence of her lover because he wanted her to divorce me, a decision requiring letters back and forth, tearful telephone calls, cautious meetings, and then the need for solitude, to roll the reality of her adventure into a small moon she could study in the palm of her hand. She said he had begged her to divorce me because he needed her in a way I did not, which made her feel needed for reasons other than the reasons she felt needed by me. His needs were new, or seemed so, because they were his, not mine, new and private needs that my wife could not share without violating the love the lovers shared, a new love accompanied by a dead trumpeter's trumpet.

As the sky darkened and night fell, my wife's voice gained confidence, becoming a voice nearly disembodied from its tale, as if it were reciting someone else's adultery. The woman I love said that if hers were only acts of infidelity, there would have been no need to confess, human frailty and attraction being what they are, but once attraction and frailty became how she fell in love, she had to confess. My wife said she had to confess so that, afterward, she could celebrate their passion. She resented feeling guilt for falling in love and resented loving me as much as she did, then resented my love for her. Her love for me, she insisted, ran so deep that being swept away by her lover had left her feeling as if she might die, and not only from guilt and fear, but also from her sexuality, which made her realize that she had been alive without breathing. *After twenty years with you*, she said, *I've forgotten how to breathe.* She knew, as soon as she experienced new love, instantly, during an orgasm, that she needed to learn again how to breathe, that she had been suffering from amnesia when it came to breathing, so that climaxes with her lover nearly killed her from breathlessness—*drowning in air*, she said. What was more, my love for her frightened her even more than hers for me, because her responsibility for my happiness had become unbearable—one of the reasons she had stopped breathing, one of the reasons she had fallen in love. *The crush of responsibility replaced breathing,* my wife said, *and I was holding my breath without knowing it.* She could remember lying motionless beside me, surprised when I would leave the room that she needed to inhale deeply, the way she inhaled her cigarette when she admitted her faithlessness on the terrace with a wineglass in her hand. She interrupted her confession to glance at me; in the glance, the stem of her wineglass was shining against the moon. From the splinter of her reflected eye, a second eye emerged, the first eye's double, the observant eye, not the eye of a participant. Then I saw my wife as a beautiful woman I did not realize had stopped breathing because of me, not the person who I assumed breathed easily with me in the room, since I did with her, at least up until now.

During her confession, I would say that desire desires nothing so much as an end to itself, turning into memory, then turning memory into the idea of desire, or the passionate contemplation of it—what my wife's adultery would leave with me after she was gone. I encouraged her to confess, no matter how disturbing her confession must be to me, in order for her to hear the words in her own voice and for me to watch her hear them, though it was growing too dark to see. Even in the darkness, when I could not see my wife's face, I could see her seeing sentences she had never formed before, her eyes wide with surprise as she spoke them, eyes I saw in the glow of her Gitanes, unblinking eyes, as if she were blind. Each moment of her confession made the adulterous acts images, then the images into thoughts, and the expression of those thoughts and images into a judgment of our marriage, then a dismemberment of our love, until our life together disappeared in my wife's impossible sentences. She sought to express a sensation, an odor, a texture—smooth, viscous, pungent—because she wanted to share her happiness and had to use words that neither of us could have imagined would refer to a lover. After my wife apologized for refusing to violate the privacy she shared with the man she loved, she violated it with enthusiasm because she enjoyed hearing herself recite the details of her impending life, enjoyed the relief of confiding her erotic secrets to the person she trusted most in the world in order to prove that there could be no going backward. Only then did I suggest that she had not been losing herself to sexual hysteria, as she believed, but that she had found herself at a sexual depth that she could only discover with someone other than me. Now that she had, we could plumb the depths together, I would say to her, lose ourselves together within the frame of my jealousy and her adultery, because jealousy, even more than adultery, liberates us to wallow in unconscionable behavior. Like adultery, jealousy acts out our direst dreams without thinking of consequences, though there are consequences. *Jealousy's sufferings are unthinkable*, I said, *until they're thought, and then they're unbearable until they're avenged.* I told my wife that I wanted to touch every inch of her body in order to know if it felt as if I had never touched it before, or as if I had touched too much of it too many times, or if it was repellent because someone else had touched it. I said I was furious that she had become an object of desire to someone other than me. I crushed my cigarette into the wall of our house so that the woman I love could see I was overcome.

Until she admitted that she had been giving serious thought to marrying her lover, my wife had been a mystery to me because of my limitless passion for her. Now she was more of a mystery and, once she was gone, my limitless passion itself would become mysterious. My insatiable desire for my wife's body remained absolute, years after I first kissed her in an elevator operated by an ageless man with Down syndrome. Undoing her Burberry, I had fluttered her labia for the first time, meaty stretched folds that opened like a book and were, I later discovered, the color of squirrel. I first put my finger into her anus in the elevator, lifting her skirt while I pressed her against the elevator wall, then sliding her panties aside in order to unlock her buttocks. From the beginning, she was the woman about whom I wanted to know and believe everything. Almost immediately, I could not imagine life without the woman I love, and I assumed she felt the same, in part because she said she did, not only when I nursed her perineum with my lips or massaged her thighs with oil, but also when we merely advanced the day, dining among acquaintances or colleagues or swimming with strangers, even though we preferred to be alone, swimming nude or dining nude. While gazing at me as I was driving, or reading, or watching a disaster unfold on television, my wife would say that she had never been happier, nor could she imagine being happier, and so she would rather die in my arms than fall in love with someone else. On the night she confessed that she was torn between remaining in our marriage and abandoning it for her lover, I knew that she could not have felt as I did, even if she had said she did because she thought she did, when we first kissed in the elevator driven by the man with Down syndrome. Even as she admitted her adultery, I wanted to immerse myself in her, just as immediately after sex I have always wanted to continue to lose myself inside my wife's body, as deeply as possible because that was as close as I could be to her mind. While my wife described her sexual ecstasy with another man, my jealousy refined itself, moving beyond her body, into a rage about her mind and how adultery had coarsened it.

In the dark, on our terrace for the last time, the woman I love murmured, *you can't imagine how terrible it's been to fall in love.* The anxiety that created the urge to fall in love had proven nothing like the anxiety of falling. *I already miss you,* I whispered. *Please,* my wife said, *I don't want to hear how you love me.* If I could have seen her face in the dark as clearly as I could hear her voice against the silence, I would have seen her eyes empty of our life together, empty of me, go blind to the history of our marriage, an emptying that would mean she had begun to experience the amnesia she needed in order to love someone else all the time and to be loved all the time by someone else. Each night, for years, we had sat on our terrace without confessing because there was nothing to confess. Now that there was, the terrace became something other than it had been, as did the darkness, as did the olive grove. Everything we saw dimly was nothing like it had ever been before, and on the next night, if I were alone on the terrace, everything would be more different. Soon, the sight of my wife would disgust me, her voice nauseate me, and, even before she left, her footfalls on the floor would sound like an intruder's. I said that I was thinking of which photograph of her to keep so I could recall her existence as time passed. The rest, twenty years of thousands of photographs, I would tear to pieces the hour of her departure, if only because she would have chosen to leave them behind. I was nostalgic for the woman who had not yet left, so I told my wife that, once she was gone, I would see her body across our bed for months on end, maybe years, motionless, belly down, a nude body disembodied from life, like evidence at a crime scene. My wife rose from her chaise to say good-bye, I assumed, or slap my face for some unfathomable reason, looming above me where I lay against a day pillow, as vulnerable physically as I was in the heart. Instead, without a word, she lifted a leg across my lap until her foot touched the floor of the terrace so that she was straddling me, staring at my face while deciding what to do next or if she ought to do what she had already decided to do, on impulse, in the heat of the moment. My wife leaned forward, pressing her weight against me, holding me in place until she was certain I would not resist, so I kissed her throat through a trellis of hair, caressing it as if I could massage the voice inside, what I most experienced during our years together, what creates and then evokes intimacy. I could see nothing because of the darkness, but I caressed my wife's skin, massaging it, as I had done for twenty years, sensing her body slip away from me, becoming a different body from the one I had known. I would forget my wife's voice once she left because, even from a distance, it had reassured me of her love, and so its absence would wound me, over and over, if I recalled it. I was losing her body, I was soon to lose her voice. I would have grasped any part of my wife's body, had she offered it in the dark, and I would have been thinking of it instead of her throat or her hair or her breasts, which she placed in my hands. I saw the shape of her, but none of the details, because only in the darkness would my wife embrace me, when no one could observe and we could not look into each other's eyes.

Own the mirror, own the reflection, my wife had said one day, studying her body after peeling away a swimsuit. She did not know I was watching from the doorway while she pinched inches of flesh from her hips unless, because of my angle of vision, I was reflected in the mirror without knowing it. On the terrace, remembering my wife squeeze her flesh as if she could pull some of it off, I realized that she must have been hiding thousands of thoughts from me, for years, awaiting someone with whom she could share them. She must have hidden them well because I never sensed anything missing. I can think as truthfully as possible about my wife and be correct some of the time, but I cannot think truthfully about myself and discover more than I already know, unless I have been lying to myself about myself, or worse, suppressing what is most significant about me, what resides in my unconscious. Perhaps only my wife could perceive what is most significant, what I have repressed, and she is leaving because of it. *Life is surrounded by death,* I said to my wife, after the confession, as she was packing a suitcase—brassieres, nylons, skirts, heels. *What about the drawer of panties?* I asked. My wife, the woman I love, laughed. *Where I'm going,* she said, *I won't need them.* Before ash, rubble, rubble subjected to thought in order to believe that there could be a moment of perfect understanding to explain my wife's exit. Whether or not, however, afterward comes nothing but ash, not a subject, not the woman I love, only residue. In twenty years of marriage, I have never *interpreted* my wife because I did not need to, or thought I did not. Suddenly, because she was leaving, she would be known to me as variations on the theme of the woman I love, of the woman I cannot help but love, as angles of complexity that rest side by side, explaining to me why or how I cannot help but love her, bringing thought to bear on the love I have felt and continue to feel, introducing anguish into my house. Smoldering ruins can occupy a panorama the way from our terrace I witness the olive grove, and the sea beyond it, and beyond the sea the horizon that cuts it, and beyond the horizon the bleeding sun, but eventually even ruin is nothing but gravity.

In the dystopia betrayal makes of love, I felt the grasp of my wife's thick thighs, a reminder of the dementia her body had enjoyed during our decades together. Even though her body was now demented on behalf of someone else, I did not risk recalling our passion to my wife because she had come to believe the future was truer than the present, that the previous decades had been a rehearsal of the truer passion she felt for the new lover, for his body instead of mine, and that their sexual acts satisfied her more than ours had. I did not want to remind her of the thinking that led to the lover's marriage proposal. In the decades of our marriage, if she straddled me, hiking her dress as she did now, baring her breasts as she did now, she would climax in seconds. Her body was so sensitive to my touch that if I put my tongue against her ear, her clitoris swelled to the size of a bean before suddenly she had an orgasm, and just as suddenly her entire body felt as if it were covered by ants. Straddling me now, she offered her throat and breasts in the dark, but I felt nothing in the folds of her thighs, even while her belly pressed mine. My wife assured herself in my ear that while she loved me, she could not remain faithful to me, no matter what she might promise, or promise to promise, because of the passion she felt for her lover. She had often remarked on her need for more mind and less flesh, but she reserved those meditations for moments after she had been sated by a sexual practice so primitive, she would say, that she feared for her humanity. Whatever the act, she would remove it from her memory until she committed it again, whatever it was, so an authentic erotic memory was already impossible before she embarked on her affair. She thought she was inventing sex because she invented the love of her life. She may have been hoping to awaken a memory of me or simply to trust her body to tell her what to do, the truest form of memory, or she may have asked her body to prove her decision right. I felt no swelling, hers or mine, and no moisture on her thighs. Under the circumstances, memory to me meant not only the failed reality of our past but also the future solitude to suffer it in.

Smothered under my wife's weight, on the chaise, on our terrace in the dark, perhaps for the last time, I was entering the museum of our marriage, or its mausoleum, in which the more I looked at our history, the less I could absorb. Though my wife was still on our terrace, holding my hips between her thighs, her face next to mine so I smelled her breath, I began to experience her body as indifferent flesh, not as the flesh I desired, but as evidence we had lived together, proof that my wife had been alive. She did not merely straddle my hips; she began to grind against me, as if we were still lovers, crushing her hips against mine, bone against bone, placing the confession in parentheses, in search of a memory, in search of attraction. She looked into my eyes, but since it was too dark to see, she traced my mouth with her thumb, making certain I was there. Before I could close my lips around her fingers, she looked away, so I could not have seen her expression even if it had been high noon. I did not know why she turned away—perhaps out of embarrassment, perhaps guilt—until I felt her pelvis press harder and faster, and I realized she was trying to find a climax by imagining her lover instead of me, seeing an image from their sexual life while straddling me instead of him. She had looked away to see her lover's face, to hide the shame of it from me. She was drawing details from memory, concentrating to paint the moment, and taking time to let a scene from their life together unfold. She would rest, breathing and imagining, then rub her flesh against what she imagined, rising up and down against my trousers, pressing the buckle of my belt into her legs. So I massaged her breasts, not to intrude, but to coax her private drama, providing the reality of flesh against flesh, but not of my flesh against hers. I urged her climax, wanting her to have it without me having mine, because she would know that I had not confused her present with her past, that she did not need to feel she had taken advantage of the only warm body in the house besides hers. To prove my loyalty, I did not speak, I did not use my voice to destroy her illusion. My wife breathed into my face, resting her forehead against mine in the dark, and suddenly relaxed her body until she whispered, for no reason other than the last gasp of intimacy, that she could do nothing to help me. She had struggled to prove our marriage must be over and had succeeded, though she breathed as heavily as she would have if the orgasm had arrived. She sat against me for several minutes, silent, but not as silent as I. When she buttoned up her breasts, I held one chill buttock until she found her balance. *You need to be ravaged*, I said, as I rubbed the inside of her thigh, *just not by me.* She stepped away from my touch and reached for her glass of wine as if it were the reason she stepped away, not the touch. Later, in the light of our threshold, as she was leaving the terrace, I saw my wife's face charged with remorse, or guilt, or perhaps surprise, or all three, or all three and more, disturbed to learn that replacing me with her lover was different from having a lover and a husband. My wife had lost her illusion when she saw her lover's face in her fantasy, saying that he would be overwhelmed if he knew she had climbed onto me in the dark. It was an observation she could make only while walking in the other direction, farther still from my touch and nearer to his. Smoking more than one Gitanes and sipping from another glass of Beaune Margaux, I suspected later that my wife was watching herself weep in the mirror above the sink, if not for the sexual impasse at which we had arrived, then for her transgression against her lover—the first betrayal of the rest of her life. The dead trumpeter's trumpet played in the kitchen. There were crickets somewhere below, frogs out there with them, bats too, eating insects when they swooped a few feet in front of me. My wife and I used to enjoy being overwhelmed by each other. Now she was overwhelmed by someone else, but suffering it. It took several minutes, alone on the terrace, in the dark, before it occurred to me that my wife dreaded my future almost as much as I did.

While I could watch my wife in the flesh, we shared a universe, where her passion and my jealousy existed side by side, or above and below. After she became invisible to me, jealousy would be only one aspect of the obsession heaping scorn and contempt on my love for the woman I love, only a part of the abjection my wife would leave in her wake. Because my wife would be invisible to me, I would be invisible to myself, needing to approach, with trepidation, a nearby mirror to remind myself I exist. That is what twenty years of sharing the universe with the woman I love will have achieved. The demeaning obsession that emerges, the scab to pick without bleeding to death, is what I would eventually think of as the ordeal of the postmortem of our marriage. Even before my wife disappeared forever, and while she rehearsed by disappearing from the terrace, whether to pack, to speak to her lover on the telephone, or to sit morbidly on the edge of our bed, I conceived the ordeal of the postmortem as the drama that would transform my jealousy into an informed despair. The compulsion to undergo the ordeal might outlast my suffering, encouraging me to exhume the corpse of my marriage, again and again, in order to slice more meat from bone, extract more marrow from bone behind the meat, find sinews I had earlier overlooked, muscle overlooked, fat. After hysterical weeping, and the false bravado of not weeping, what could the ordeal achieve other than preserving the corpse of my marriage in ether, proving to me that I had loved my wife to death—mine, not hers. During the ordeal, I would be not only the husband my wife rejected but also an observer of the rejection, relentlessly addressing the subject as an outsider hoping to escape doom by understanding it from those who did not. By abandoning our marriage, my wife would make me an object to myself, my own *otherness*, replacing no less than herself as the otherness in my life. I did not so much conceive the ordeal of the postmortem as have it descend upon me, in the face of insurmountable grief, as inevitable as it was instantaneous, teaching me that human beings are primordially prepared to accommodate catastrophe because they immediately wonder how they will survive, not how they will succumb.

Saying she loved me differently, but not less, since she had fallen in love with someone else, my wife confessed that it was easier for her to love me now that there was nothing she needed. *I love you as you are, maybe for the first time,* she said, *because you have nothing I want. You're a wonderful husband.* I selected excruciating moments to remind my wife of what had been a ravenous love between us and an empathy in the face of fear and failure, the empathy and passion more than accidents of time and space, more than familiarity and restlessness. *What do you feel for me?* I asked without thinking, asking the question that should not be asked of someone in love with someone else elsewhere. My wife sighed, vexed, so I waved the idea away and started a cigarette in order to hear the match snap and then to see the fire strike against the night sky. My wife pouted her lips because she decided to think, in spite of her desire not to, for an answer to my question, which I regretted having asked. I said I regretted it, but even my wife was curious to articulate her feelings about me because she had spent an inordinate time articulating her feelings about the lover. She looked into the far dark distance for words swimming by. My mistake had been grave, so I watched my wife's mouth begin to form a sentence I did not want to hear and she did not want to utter, which were the reasons she needed to reply. *Affection,* she said, pleased with her accuracy, *abiding affection,* but not passion now that she knew what it truly was and where it was located. The woman I love folded her hands and pointed the steeple of her fingers at her lower belly, as if I knew nothing about what was there. I reminded her that she had ejaculated thousands of times during our marriage, that we had ejaculated simultaneously hundreds of times, that no body part had been spared our ejaculates. *All these ejaculations must embarrass you,* I said, *especially those in which you ejaculated because of me.* My wife said she did not think of them, that once she had fallen in love, she forgot our sexual life completely, and in particular which acts we performed, though she admitted that our sexual life must have influenced her new one because her lover was grateful that my wife enjoyed as much as she enjoyed, knew what she knew, and was not burdened by hygiene or limits.

In the den of a bistro, near the metro, it was my wife, my wife said, not the lover, who directed his fingers to her labia, and where, within seconds, she had achieved her most intense climax in years, puddling the chair on which she sat. *The chair was so wet,* she said, *we had to move to another table, and the couple that sat down where we had sat complained to the waiter that someone must have spilled a glass of beer.* If the world does not come to an end after my wife deserts me, then I will be a man who is waiting for the world to come to an end, and that would mean being a man for whom the world is irreparable. If the world does not come to an end when my wife leaves me, I will be forced to live with the certitude that it will, that the anxiety I am bearing must end with the end of the world as I know it. Until it ends, I cannot forget that it has not ended and that because the woman I love has left, I am forced to relive how our marriage died and was dismembered by my wife. My wife and I had enjoyed our marriage to the exclusion of everything that was not it. Our love had no boundaries, but for the world. *Marriage ends at the puddle's edge,* I said to the woman I love after she confessed that she, not he, had been the aggressor, even revealing to him one of her breasts in a station of the metro, at midnight, as the metro roared in, which is what led the lovers to a bistro near the metro. While my wife's abandonment of our marriage meant for me that the world would end, or that I could do nothing but wait for the world to end, for her the world had to continue because she had fallen in love, a love that would continue after the world that I was waiting to end ended. I told my wife that I could forgive everything, even anything, except that deserting our marriage had caused me to become a victim of *the meaning of life.*

Time meant nothing, so that nothing I experienced during the confession could be measured by sun or moon, including my wife's disappearance from the terrace, a significant space but, nonetheless, timeless. During my wife's absence, I placed my sunglasses across my eyes, even though the horizon was already darker than the bottom of a boot. It was her absence I needed my sunglasses for, not the moonlight, and not the landscape below, which, without seeing it, I knew contained wads of bostryx, a bolus of crushed olive, the spavine trunks of trees, rabbits, vermin, the usual rodentia. The sunglasses I wore emphasized the catastrophe that my wife postponed by deserting the terrace, which I was left to contemplate alone in the dark, contemplate the awesome meaning of, not the trivial meaning of a trivial truth, such as in which bistro beside which station of the Paris metro my wife first placed a stranger's finger on the hood of her cowbell. I not only wore the sunglasses against the end of our intimacy, but as a screen for thought, preparing myself, by leaning back in my chaise, crossing my ankles, and looking into the dark from behind dark glasses, to hear in my wife's revised voice worse than the worst thing I could imagine hearing. Because I could see less than nothing, the sunglasses anticipated her disappearance, leading me to transform it into a previously unknown state of being, a dissolution of human cells out of a glandular science fiction. If there was a warning that twenty years after we fell in love, my wife would fall out of it in order to fall in it elsewhere, with someone else, it would have been that after our first matinee, lasting three days, she immediately had another, hoping to prove the inauthenticity of ours. When sex with someone else the same week proved to be only sex with someone other than me, the woman I love telephoned with the happy news that while she had enjoyed a convulsive and howling orgasm with an architect, whose penis was as thick as her wrist, it had not meant a thing. There were other humorous efforts to escape being in love with me, including China. *I must have been insane,* she said when she returned.

While I have always been intrigued by what my wife has had to say on any subject, I have often been mystified by what she has neglected to say. She would often stop a sentence, stopping a thought in the middle of the thought, or the sentence, often just before I expected the salient moment to arrive from her mouth. Nothing did instead. When nothing did instead, I would assume she assumed I knew how to finish the thought without her, the way other couples would ask each other which dishes on a menu they prefer, as if overtaken in a restaurant by galloping senility. Since our intimacy must have meant that we were more alike than not, more like each other than others were like us, I was presumed to be able to complete her thought silently, as if she had continued speaking, more or less gathering what I would have thought she was going to say. For instance, during her confession, she said that she used to imagine growing old with me, then she went silent. Soon she left the terrace, and by the time I finished her thought, I could hear the murmur of her voice, murmuring to herself in the bathroom or on the telephone, murmuring to Paris. Though she assumed I could infer the end of her sentence after she left the terrace so that the unfinished thought's inference would be obvious to me by the time she returned, my ability to finish her thoughts and sentences, like hers to finish mine, did not mean I could conclude I knew her, or she me. As I awaited her return, I concluded that inferring each other's thoughts had obviously not included *all* thoughts, and inferred sentences did not preclude concealed infidelities or other thoughts neither complete nor incomplete, so the perfect intimacy conferred by inferred endings to each other's thoughts and sentences was provably untrue. Even though the woman I love constituted the content of most of my thinking, most of the day any day, it occurred to me, in the dark, on our terrace, that rather than knowing her because of all this thinking about her, my assumption of intimacy had made me an accomplice to her adultery. *When I wash my face in the morning,* I would tell my wife as soon as she returned, *a few memories remind me of who I am, and new tasks for the day suggest how I might be changed by evening.* I examine my face dripping with soap and water, as I have done all my life and every day for twenty years; after I have wiped my eyelids clear of water, I see my wife's face beside mine in the mirror, whether she is there or not. I would say this to my wife when, and if, she returned to the terrace. Though my pulse rate might vary, I would say to the woman I love, because of her face beside mine in the morning and at night, the fingerprints remain the same. *I know who I am because I know* you, I would say to my wife of twenty years. It occurred to me, waiting for her to return, that despite our intimacy, or even because of our intimacy, I did not know the woman I love at all but had been deluded by spending days and nights together, for years and years, assuming that we could not live together every day for two decades without knowing each other completely, authentically, especially if one or the other of us presumed we could finish each other's thoughts or sentences. Once it occurred to me we could have spent twenty years together, every day and every night, without knowing each other at all, I wondered if the woman I love had ever been the woman I should have married, or if I should have married anyone, ever. Though I had had lovers before I met the woman I love, once I met her, I could not account for my existence before we met. I know who I am because I am married to the woman I love. If she were to leave me for the lover, it would be because she viewed her life as meaningful without me and that she had come to view her life with me as inauthentic, false, or lacking conviction. Because she now saw that our life of twenty years was based on false consciousness, she could conclude that I would be better off without her, as she without me, free to seek an authentic consciousness, maybe someone even younger, slimmer, smarter, maybe taller, shorter, less buxom, less hippy, just anyone except her, with her myriad flaws and weaknesses, about which I had never before heard, including her failure to finish thoughts and sentences, suddenly not a strength, but a sign of our incompatibility. By leaving, she was doing me a favor, she said, or inferred, by refusing to complete the sentence concerning old age.

While waiting for my wife to confess her decision to leave, it occurred to me that, immediately after we married, my wife was nothing like she said she would be. I thought, at the time, how self-deluded she is to believe she is one sort of person when it is obvious to anyone she is not, though not so deluded as to be the opposite of who she thinks she is. Once, she said, she expected me to fall in love with another woman and leave her, because she knew she was not the person she had said she would be, or become, after our marriage. My newlywed wife assumed that someone as passionate as I was, and am, would desert someone like her once I discovered how little she understood her own passions and how poorly she could articulate her deepest needs. *I'm visual,* my wife liked to say, *not verbal.* She believed that I would leave her once my ambitions in the external world began to be realized so that I could realize the passions of my private life as well. Within a few years of telling me this, my wife began to be successful in her career, then noteworthy, and now it was she, not I, who had fallen in love and was about to leave. She said at the time of our wedding, twenty years before she fell in love with someone other than me, that she expected one day I would leave her for someone more interesting and beautiful, which meant to me, twenty years later, since she had now fallen in love, that she must have concluded the new lover was more interesting and more handsome than I. She thought, at the outset of our marriage, that she could not survive the world without me and was grateful I felt the same way about her, which meant she must now have concluded she could not survive the world with me, or not without her new lover, and therefore could not survive the world if she were forced by her conscience, or entropic weight, rather than at gunpoint, for example, to remain married to me. I was preparing to loathe the woman I love and despise her existence, wishing she had never been born because I could have been happy with a different woman, in a different universe of possibilities, who would not, after decades of marriage, be deserting me for a new lover, let alone reminding me of misgivings about herself that she had expressed the day of our marriage because her misgivings were now proving convenient. However, I could not imagine an emotional disease that would allow me to love the woman I love as deeply as I do, for as long as I have, and will, unless she loved me in return. I would be conjuring the nude image of my wife decades into the future, knowing that at the same moment she was not conjuring my nude image, that she would not have given a thought to me after she packed and left for her new life in Paris. Hearing the dead trumpeter's trumpet beside my wife's voice murmuring in the dark, I had begun to bathe in an idea of erotic eternity in which the woman I love, by her absence, would forever be the nude woman I love, never more desirable, never to age as I would age. *I should have taken your nipples between my lips while I still could,* I would tell my wife as soon as she returned.

Whatever else you can expect if you desert me, I would say to my wife when she returned to the terrace, *I will see you nude on the chaise; nude in the kitchen; nude, and on display, across our bed; nude in rooms in which you have never been nude; and nude in public, day after day and night after night. Nude, tattooed, and sexually available, no matter where you travel, or reside, once you leave our house. It will drive a nail into your skull,* I would tell my wife, *to know that no matter how far from me you think you can travel, you'll always be within the walls of our house, oiled, nude, provocative.* Maybe not knowing herself was the reason my wife married me, either to feel protected because I did know myself, whatever that means, or because she believed she had found a kindred spirit, who did not know himself any better than she knew herself. In her confession, my wife insisted that she did not know why she was doing what she was doing. Until her confession, my wife would not have acknowledged the flaw in her iris, let alone in her character. Because she fell in love with adultery, the adultery became a romance, so not knowing herself was both the explanation for falling in love and its reward. I would explain that since I did know myself, whatever that means, once she left our house, I would see her in it, night and day, year after year, nude and seductive and always sexually available, always on display, but if she preferred I think of her as *emotionally bereft* as well, as my wife characterized her condition, I would include it in the subtitles of the film comprising the ordeal of the postmortem. My nude faithless wife, her hundreds of lovers.

As a curtain of moonlight rumpled the lap of my trousers, which I mistook for the woman I love turning on a tall reading lamp inside the house, I was surrounded by silence. No trumpet, no running water, no whispers, no frogs, crickets, or neighboring dogs. The surround was as deprived of sound as an unlit room at midnight is deprived of light, the unlit room about which the philosopher asks if the roses in it are still red. It was a preposterous silence, a silence piercing my ears as a dog whistle pierces the dog's, a silence that choked me, so I was choking on the decision of my wife to expose me to the noise I could expect to hear once she was gone: the noise of nothing, of absolutely nothing, in a room as dark as a bedroom at midnight, unless a dish of moonlight bathes the room ash gray so that the stillness evokes, even more, what is missing from it. After asking my wife if she had ever loved me during our decades together, she said that in order to fall in love a second time, she had had to fall in love a first. I had been the first, though before she fell in love with me, she had thought, on one or two occasions, that she had fallen in love with others. It is possible, I thought in the new moonlight and the new silence on our terrace, that the woman I love has never loved anyone, including me, and including the new lover, that she is incapable of love, or she calls anyone who supports her worldly ambitions a loved one, confusing her self-absorption with the ability to experience love. It was not that she did not love me as much as, or in the ways, I loved her, but that I loved her despite the fact that she was not, or no longer, very lovable. I told her from the terrace in a loud voice, *you aren't very lovable*. She was sensual, smart, talented, which usually means, as it did in her case, that she was not particularly lovable, not empathetic, though like most unlovable talented people, she demanded empathy from others all the time. Her confession devastated me because it meant she was even less lovable than I had thought, less than I had come to accept, less lovable than I was lovable. I am not lovable, but I realized, sitting alone on the terrace, that I could not have remained lovable living with someone, for twenty years, who is not. No matter how completely I thought I knew her, I had not known how different we were. *We're different people,* she said during the confession, meaning that while she and I were suddenly different, she and the new lover were suddenly similar, if not exactly the same. *We're incompatible,* my wife said, *not only different.* Her new life was going to celebrate compatible love, a love never truer than when lovers say, as my wife said on our terrace, *ours is a mad love, perhaps doomed, but beautiful. Mad and doomed,* she said proudly, as if mad and doomed existed without doomed mad human beings who are faithless, or as if beautiful love was the reward.

I was eager to ask the woman I love if, in the presence of her lover, the man she suddenly could not imagine living without, the world became a different world because he was in it and I was not. My wife said she could no longer imagine life with me, which meant that the world we had created, then inhabited together, had failed her. When she said during the confession, *I don't know what I want,* I realized that she knew what she wanted and I was not going to be happy about it. I was eager to tell my wife that it was possible she had fallen in love because she believed we had come to understand each other too well, had finished too many of each other's sentences and thoughts. If she had come to dread how well I knew her, or how profoundly I understood her fears, anxieties, and flaws, and hoped to enjoy decades with another husband until she would dread what he knew of her, I wanted to say that she need not dread anything at all. I could confess, in the middle of her confession, that after twenty years, I had no idea who the woman I love was, even if she knew everything of me. *We may as well be at the beginning,* I was eager to tell her. *As far as I know,* I wanted to say, *you and I have just met.* I was eager for the woman I love to return to our terrace so I could wonder aloud if she had fallen in love in order to return mystery to the present, if the first moment of her betrayal seemed a mysterious event, nothing like the past, with nothing but future. I wanted to tell my wife I believed that, at the moment she betrayed our love for each other, her husband of two decades became the foremost distant object, in time and space, while the new lover obliterated the certainty of sickness and death. I was a past love, and so my wife obliterated me as a breathing human being in need of her as she had been in need of me. The loss of my wife would leave me vanquished by the physical world, my only sensations reduced to suffering her loss. In the future, my sense of the physical world would consist of the anxiety I suffer concerning my fate in it without her. In order to experience physical sensation, other than my wife's absence, I would need to slice off a foot, for instance, or a hand, another, so that the misery I knew reflexively, each hour, each day, could be overwhelmed by an observable wound. Short of losing a limb, no sensation could have meaning in the ordeal of the postmortem of my failed marriage, no meaning other than to recall that my wife and I would never touch again, not just that I would never fibrillate her clitoris, or erect her nipples, or massage her buttocks before opening them, but neither would I kiss her shoulder in passing, or rub her feet at night, or wash her hair over the kitchen sink. The suffering of the ordeal of the postmortem would be undetectable because my body would feed on itself, organ by organ, internals desiccating until they mortified, forbidding me from taking a step without keeling over onto my shadow. The wound that slowly brings the body to a close never itself closes, never scabs, or it leaves an excoriation of proud flesh to symbolize having survived the worst the human being closest to me could have achieved. Every moment will feel like the end of the world, but in the next moment the world will not have ended, until the next moment in which it also does not end, neither ending nor not ending, there being nothing to alleviate the certainty that if it is not ending now, the world will end immediately.

The end of the world is the next thing to happen because it is the only thing that has not happened.

The first time I ejaculated into my wife's mouth, while she ejaculated into mine, we were certain our future would be blissful—infused by talent, intelligence, and thousands of orgasms. Twenty years later, the same themes have produced our ruin. Everything was fine before the creation of the universe, I would tell my exuberant wife when she reassured me how liberating my liberation would soon feel. Her smirk, the first smirk I had seen since the confession began, in fact the first smirk in the history of our marriage, confirmed my fear that nothing I could say would persuade my wife of anything unless it served her interest, which could not serve mine. *I have never seen you smirk*, I said. *How long have you been smirking behind my back?* I asked. *How long have you been thinking in smirks when you hear my voice?* I asked my wife of twenty years. *How long have you concealed your hostility?* She opened her arms to apologize, as if I still had a mother, then constructed a sentence in the passive—*I want you to know you're still loved. By whom?* I asked. I waved my wife's maternal grasp out of the way, telling her I feared being touched by hands that had touched her lover's penis. *I prefer not to risk bacteria*, I said. Another smirk, the second smirk in twenty years of marriage, but this time unapologetic and dramatic, authentic, ruthless. My wife deserted the terrace, raising the alarm that she was about to desert our house, to desert our marriage, me. I would be forced to remember a smirk, her first, as her final expression, to me an inescapable opinion concerning our decades together. After she has left, I thought, if the cowbell rings below, and it is not my wife returning, the sound of the cowbell will disturb me for days because I will always almost hear it. So, too, the telephone. If the telephone rings, without my wife causing it, exhaustion for days on end, anxiety, insomnia, and exhaustion for days and days because inanimate objects from our marriage, from our mutual delusion—assuming the delusion was not only mine—will betray me as much as the woman I love has betrayed me, being conspicuously themselves, yet different, conspicuously the cowbell following my wife's departure, the telephone since she has fled, the bath towel she will never again wrap around her luxurious nudity, recalling my wife's disappearance whenever I am in their presence or they in mine. Stretched out on the chaise, during a silence broken only by the flight of bats across a soft dog's moon, I felt the way I had felt when, because we were separated, I convinced myself that my wife had forgotten I existed. When the woman I love was in Sri Lanka, St. Petersburg, or Berlin promoting the exhibition of her works, weeks could pass before I received so much as a postcard, and if I telephoned her hotel or leased apartment, I invariably spoke to a machine or had to ask a clerk to leave my wife a message. Often the clerk's hesitation or the tone of his voice made me believe he was lying beside my wife at that moment, that I had not reached the desk in the lobby but my wife's hotel room, an absurd notion suggesting how my wife's neglect unnerved me. I did not think she was having an affair with a desk clerk or that a lover was pretending to be a desk clerk if I telephoned, but her indifference when we were not together reminded me of the indifference of someone in the throes of an affair. I had begun to worry that my wife routinely had affairs in foreign hotels and that desk clerks had been paid to convince me she did not. Not once in the years of her climb to success in the art world had she answered a telephone when I called, but in order to promote herself and her works, in order to have become a success as an artist, she must have answered hundreds of other people's telephone calls. Other people would not have taken an interest in her career if she repeatedly ignored their telephone calls. Her silence, for weeks, caused me to spend our time apart wondering what she was doing without me instead of living my days and weeks away from her in much the same way as I spent them with her. Because of her indifference to my concern regarding her indifference to my existence, life experience ceased to exist for me when the woman I love and I were apart, not because I could not bear to be away from her, but because she might have been kidnapped by sheiks who enjoyed whipping buxom Western women until they were dead.

On occasion, my wife's disrespectful silence and neglect caused me to withdraw from the world, so while she was away, I might not speak to anyone other than a service person for weeks. I wanted to make certain I would be home if she telephoned, not so much because I wanted to talk to her or to know how her career was going at the moment or to remind her that I missed her nude body beside me, but in order to ask why she was ignoring me, as she invariably promised she would not do before leaving on every one of her careerist excursions. I would sit first in one chair, then another, then sit up in bed because it was bedtime, passing whole days and nights, expressing disappointment and ire to my invisible wife at her stunning indifference. My reclusiveness led to insomnia, the insomnia to despair, so each dawn I would look out over the olive grove in my bathrobe, massaging the stubble on my chin and cheeks, and observe a fog above the sea's surface as if it were a toxic vapor rising from the earth's core. My insomnia would begin because I invariably thought I was being burgled in the night, and once I convinced myself I was not, I realized I had awakened because in my fitful sleep I thought I had heard my wife returning home. *Not felons, but the woman I love,* I would say to the mirror, where I rinsed the danger from my face. I must have dreamed that she returned, despite the late hour, because she was desperate to be reunited, but I would have been awakened by a knowledge within the dream that the dream was a lie, the way I used to be awakened because I was about to land in the street after being sucked from the window of an airplane. Sleep was supposed to refresh me, even to refresh my concerns over my wife's indifference, to prove my concerns were nothing but loneliness, but dreams about her exhausted me because I knew them to be true. As soon as I thought my wife had returned, then realized that she had not, I could not sleep because I was hurt and angry that she had not, nor would she tell me, if later I reached her, when it was that she would.

When my wife first left to arrange or to attend one of her exhibitions, a decade before she fell in love with someone else, I enjoyed the solitude and enjoyed missing her, remembering what her presence meant to me, indulging the loneliness that made me feel calm and wise, reclusive rather than lonely, that prepared me to be a better person once she returned home. Occasionally, I hoped my wife would remain longer than she did so that I could appreciate her presence even more. Gradually, however, the separations bewildered me. As the separations grew longer, as she was more and more absent, she would return home just as distant from me as if she were still gone. Her physical absence had proved difficult when it lasted for several weeks, but when she was home, and still remained absent to me, it was insufferable. She would accuse me of having turned into an unwashed unshaven hermit in order to punish her, of not engaging the world when she was absent in order to sabotage her career. Each absence was longer than the previous one, and for several years I hoped they would change the woman I love so that when she returned, she would be fully present to me. That way, even as the absences grew longer and the distances greater (her career was flourishing, multilingual), I could still look forward to her return without worrying that one day she would forget to come home. But when she returned and was not fully present, was not more present than before she had left, her presence made things worse, including my intuition that while she was absent she had had to convince herself she was missing me but upon her return was disappointed to find that she had not missed me at all. When we were apart, I suspected she was *trying* to miss me, *hoping* she would be eager to return, but once she was home she would also be disappointed because she realized she preferred where she had been to where she was, and that while she had been away, she had been dreading coming home. When she returned home, not fully present, she immediately began new work that would take her away as soon as it was completed, a way of being cheerful and optimistic around the house, instead of being full of dread because she was in it. When she first traveled to promote her career, my wife would return ravenous for my flesh, unable to wait until she showered, or ate, or napped before reclaiming my body as her property or as a missing feature of her body as her body was a missing piece of mine. Even before I would see her, I would hear her enter the house, after which I would see, instead of the woman I love, a trail of clothes leading from the door to our bedroom, a trail beginning with her maroon Burberry, then shoes and a blouse, followed by a big brassiere and sometimes, and sometimes not, a thin strip of colorful panties, depending upon whether she had worn panties during the train journey home. On rare occasions, if I was at the door when she returned, my wife would say nothing before bending across one of our winged armchairs, hiking her skirt, and opening an orifice with her fingers. As years and journeys continued, as my wife's career drew crowds of sightseers, our separations fired her imagination in startling directions, which I enjoyed but would have enjoyed more had I not been baffled. Who would surprise their spouse, after twelve married years, with the tattoo of a Hindu goddess on her belly, inches above her ovaries? Who would return home, after a month in Berlin, hairless at her foramen, like a newborn? A paddle, but not for a canoe, rested in her suitcase, beside a riding crop, though we owned no pony. Eventually, I awaited my wife's surprises with the anxiety that they did not correspond to the woman I love as I had known her for years and years. We enacted her fantasies with muted success, each of them eagerly attempted but quickly abandoned, reminding us that fantasies are for the mind instead of the body, promising a future in which to act them, postponing death the way pornography fixes sexual release for all time. In the months before her confession, as eager as ever to take initiative, my wife would overwhelm me when she returned so that our reunions were on her terms, salacious terms that I grew to realize meant satisfying me with her hands or her mouth, but, as if it were the rule of a game, I was not allowed to touch her, and she would remain clothed, often in the crisp maroon Burberry. She assured me it was a fantasy she shared—a strange woman, her body hidden in a coat, satisfying a man as quickly as possible. Before I could disagree, my wife's lips or fingers would have surrounded my penis to the root, and I would stop thinking, sensation interrupting thought, or postponing it, or enhancing it, as well as the sadness of it—whatever happens when you feel the arrival of a loveless sexual release. I would miss the days when she had surprised me with handcuffs or something that might electrocute us.

On my chaise, in the silent dark, awaiting my wife's unfinished confession, I understood this to be the beginning of the most important event of my life. I had begun the most overwhelming experience I would ever know other than the onset of my death, should I have the time to know it, assuming this was not its beginning. The realization of the calamity *unfolded*, inviting an onslaught of mortifying mental events and a narrative of absolute ruin, with no one to witness it but myself, the ruined. Because my wife could not endure our marriage another day, she knew that I would intuit the misery I was about to experience and that I, even in my shock, would already begin to suffer the anxiety of dreading the misery after she was gone. I could begin to dread the inevitability of the misery and how miserable it might grow to be, though I could not know how dreadful my misery would become. I permitted my wife to know me completely over twenty years, and, as a result, she decided that she would prefer to know someone else instead. Her confession would be the first paragraph of my personal disaster, I thought while I smoked and sipped wine on the chaise, on the terrace, in the pallor of the dog's moon. My first paragraph of the catastrophe has arrived, I thought, but it was my wife's last, the story she had been building for weeks, a story I had been observing her build. The confession erased adulterous acts in favor of profound emotions, as if her passionate new love bore the gravity of ours, translating lustful symptoms of mental woe into dreamboats of hope. The confession, as far as it went before my wife announced an intermission, had read like the first paragraph of an argument, the same way that, when I sliced a thin edge of cheese, I considered it less than a wedge, and then I considered that I was sliding into my mouth a short paragraph of cheese. I would tell my wife that once she has left I will constantly see her nude, oiled, and erotically charged, to implant in her the same self-consciousness I would suffer. My nightly and daily hallucination of my wife as sexually vulnerable and insatiable would serve as an obstacle in her daily life to the wanton happiness she expected from her permanent state of infidelity. *You won't be able to disrobe in front of him*, I said, *without feeling my hand driving the zipper, nor will you splay your legs across the room from him, for him, one leg across one wing of an armchair, the other leg the other wing, without seeing me seated beside him, watching you do it. As for fellatio, as for cunnilingus,* I said to my wife, leaving the sentence where it sat.

The ordeal would be the most meaningful experience of my life, more meaningful than my twenty-year marriage, which will have come to an end, because minutiae, nonsense, and the pointless will gather meaning to themselves without becoming something else, not until the world comes to an end. If my marriage gave unspoken meaning to my life, its absence would leave my life meaningless but for an understanding of the nature of meaning and the nature of the meaningless. *Make no mistake,* I said to myself in the dark, *the ordeal will appear each day like a smoking deathscape, a world destroyed by plague or nuclear winter.* Even sunset on the sea beyond the olive groves will not be spared. The ordeal of our failed marriage will mean that a lifetime of anxiety had at last found an adequate subject. Catastrophe came into existence on the terrace of our house in the country because the darkness and silence surrounding me were nothing like they had been the night before. If someone had asked me to describe them, I would not have used the same words *darkness* and *silence* that I used the night before. Nothing I saw, or could have seen, or heard, or could have heard, would have prepared me the day before for the different understandings I would have of *silence* and *darkness* the next day, in the next darkness and silence. Perhaps the first among thousands of details of my undoing that was only beginning to unfold, the transformation of silence and darkness made my flesh crawl—not only crawl, but feel pins and needles and ache as well, as if I had been stricken with a historic influenza. I was at once paralyzed and in pain, chained to the chaise by my wife's absence and by her silence. Because she is gone from the terrace, I thought in my paralysis, she is also silent, even if she is whispering on the telephone to her lover in Paris from our bedroom. I wanted to tell my wife of my pain and paralysis and of my fear that while I suffered them she was speaking to her lover about the confession, informing her lover of how I was accepting her new reality and receiving from him the encouragement to continue or to finish her explanation so they could celebrate her freedom from our marriage. I wanted to warn my wife of my paralysis and pain, but I could not speak either. I could not have spoken any more than I could have moved. My wife, speaking to Paris and moving her legs in order to massage her clitoris to the sound of her lover's exhortations, was able to move and speak, but I was not. Had there been a massive fire on the terrace, I would have been charred where I sat, charred in the chaise that would have melted into my flesh, the crawling and aching flesh that the woman I love was about to leave in her wake. Once I concluded that the darkness and silence were nothing like they were the night before the beginning of my wife's confession and would become still stranger to me in the future, I could not escape the onslaught of altered realities constituting the collapse of my nexus not only with the world I had known for the twenty years of our marriage, but also with the world I had known before our marriage. Because I had been able to comprehend how my life before my wife entered it had prepared me to be, among other things, her husband, I could account for most of my life as a meaningful experience. It had, over twenty years, seemed natural and inevitable that my wife and I should have met, fallen in love, and married, when of course, as I could now plainly see, there had been nothing natural or inevitable about it. Whether I considered myself frozen or melted onto my chaise during the first night of the new darkness and new silence, I suspected there were millions of misunderstandings to reveal in the future of the disaster that had only just begun, and *nothing but* millions of misunderstandings, *nothing but* confirmations that there had never been anything natural or inevitable about falling in love, or marrying my wife, or remaining married for twenty years any more than it was inevitable and natural that the love would have ended, and in its place there would be jealousy, regret, enmity. I knew that the first night of the catastrophe was not a dream because, if it had been, now was the moment I should have awakened, when silence and darkness were nothing like they were outside the dream, or before the dream, or within the self-consciousness that might have reminded me, during the dream, that what I was living was only a dream.

I eagerly awaited the return of my wife so that she could view the debris I had become because of her. It was possible, I thought in my mute and paralyzed condition, that her reappearance might return my speech and motion to me, that since her absence left me with no one to speak to and no one to touch, I had been able to do neither. She had given me a deliberately cruel measure of time in which to acquaint myself with life in her absence, what she might have believed was a merciful preparation for the impact of our finish. Even if my wife did not know herself as well as I knew myself, as she conveniently claimed, or said she did not because she knew herself better than I knew myself, or thought she did, she knew the impact of her confession on my future, on the images of her that have comprised the core of my existence for two decades, my erotic milieu. My erotic milieu had been *our* erotic milieu. Waiting for my wife to return, and without as yet a scar of detail, I began to experience the reality of the unreality of my existence once she was gone. After her departure to the arms of another man, mine would be a nonexistence. My nonexistence would consist of what was missing from my existence, of enumerating for days on end all that her departure had taken from me, enumerating, and nothing more, once she will have departed—*débouched*, she would remark in her confession. I experienced the reality of the unreality of the nonexistence I could see on the horizon; altered darkness, silence, mute paralysis, and crawling flesh already forming more nonexistence than I could live with, even for a short time, let alone the days, weeks, and months I would live with it. I did not anticipate being touched again by another human being. As for the silence around me and the muteness that enhanced the silence, they shattered the intimate language of love my wife and I had constructed over decades, the proof, each day, of our difference from the objective universe. I could not allow myself to think of our private speech, of our marriage's intimate diction, because I was about to be the lone speaker of it. I presumed the transformations of *darkness* and *silence* pointed me toward the future dead speech of my marriage. As if there had been a coup while a nation slept, the language of my marriage was suddenly illegitimate. My wife could not believe in the reality of her new love if she did not believe in the unreality of the old. The new reality required a new language that envisioned a new world, a new way of seeing, a way that must begin as an alternative vision to the vision she would have mastered over twenty years and which now would be displaced, or even erased, because she had come to suffer rather than enjoy it, concluding that the vision had been false compared to the new needs embodied in the new reality. Perhaps *darkness* and *silence* were different for my wife too, but she enjoyed the difference. From the difference my wife was choosing, I would be relegated to the past, in fact defining the past from the view of my wife's personal history. In the context of a new view of the world, our marriage would constitute a barbaric prehistory. In order for my wife's new personal life to define her present, the past would have to become a past that was burned to a cinder on behalf of civilization. Even an incidental thought of me in the future would be the inexplicable imprint of a cave dweller.

Every few seconds, the end of my cigarette glowed like a firefly because I was deep in thought—Gitanes between two fingers, glass of wine between two others, the rest of me paralyzed and speechless. My wife's long absence from the terrace was, for her, an absence from nothing, the terrace and her chaise on it nothing, the wine we drank nothing, her husband nothing. Wherever she was in our house, she noted nothing, noted nothing everywhere, anywhere, all around her nothing, until nothing characterized the past that was, even now, becoming distant past, and therefore more nothing than it was the day before. Even if she thought she was seeing something, in her heart of hearts she knew she was seeing nothing or something glued to the remote past and so as good as nothing. She would leave me nothing for my nonexistence, assuming she knew she was leaving. Nothing made everything impossible, anything too, so that eventually I would face the irrefutable truth that only my nonexistence existed, that anything and everything else were impossible. Knowing me as well as she did, which was as well as she could after twenty years, my wife knew that this would be the state of being she would leave in her wind. The nonexistence, packed with nothing, illustrated a horizon before me, the way the low wall of my terrace illustrates a horizon, beyond which lies the sea's horizon, where the sun does not so much rise in the morning as invade the empty space above the clean line of the planet. But for the sun, the planet would be free. I understood my wife's prolonged absence and silence as proof that she understood the unspeakable condition I would find myself in once she abandoned our marriage, that she understood the consequences for me even if she did not know the consequences for herself. The more she suggested that her decision could be the worst of her life, the more I prepared for the worst of mine because my wife repeated her sentence many times to assuage me, as if I would have more of a future than she, which I did not believe she believed any more than I did. I had not fallen madly in love. During my wife's absence from the terrace, I met the nonexistence of my future because the intimate speech of our marriage ceased to have meaning. I may as well have finished my wife's confession or could now understand that she had left the terrace because she could not speak to me the way she had spoken for twenty years, that she spoke differently because she was in love with someone else, in a different universe. It was as if my wife had forgotten her native language, though she might have said she had only now remembered it and had been living as a foreigner for twenty years, as if she had been shipwrecked with me, a stranger from the start. *I'm in anguish*, my wife said before she left the terrace. Her anguish was that of living a discontinuous life, she said, a source of panic. Because of its intensity, her anguish made her resent not only our marriage but her adultery as well. *I can't account for the sensations when I'm with him*, my wife said, *which is why I feel helpless to do anything but succumb as he's succumbing to me. There's nothing I won't do to end the anguish*, the woman I love said. My wife had earlier carped that our marriage had swallowed her, which was why the affair began, but now that the affair had swallowed her, she realized our marriage had not, and that being swallowed whole had been what was missing from it. I admired my wife's suffering. *I wish I were in your place*, I said, *instead of mine. That's how much I love you*, I added, before she left me alone on the terrace.

Sex with him has been wonderful, my wife said, *more than wonderful. Sex like ours*, she continued, tapping her fingernail against her wineglass, *has to mean something more than sex; at least that's how it feels when he and I come together, as if the sex gets in the way of the spirit, as if my ejaculations are more than gushing ejaculations, and not only because he's coming gushes too.* Her fingernail continued tapping the glass, suggesting that her memory was making her thighs itch. My wife could not remember the number of climaxes she had enjoyed the first time she had enjoyed them at a bistro with a trumpet like our radio's trumpet and, later, on the filthy floor of her studio in the Bastille. *I felt wanton and entitled*, my wife said about being massaged to an orgasm in the corner of a jazz club. *In the morning*, she said, *I had a hangover that made his semen taste salty, so I wasn't sure I wanted to see him again. He phoned a day later, and the moment I heard his voice, I knew I would see him again.* I told the woman I love, before she left me to the misery of thinking through my misery until I was paralyzed and mute, that I loved her so deeply I would continue to desire her after I no longer could bear the thought of her. *I love you so much*, I said, *I wish I liked you. If you want to be free of your anguish*, I told my wife, *keep devastation on your mind at all times.* When I arrived at the simplest understanding of my future without the woman I love, I uncorked another Beaune Margaux because the first rested on the tile floor, empty and opaque, held in place by a handful of moonlight. I uncorked loudly, tempting my wife to return, reminding her that opening a bottle of wine, in the dark of the night, had been throughout our marriage a sexual invitation. I was as sober as a corpse, however, indicating that the trauma of the death of my marriage had begun, that my body was burrowing into terror and jealousy, then deeper, into regret and rage, which gradually would open onto a vast space of self-loathing over the dread I could not avoid because of my loss. If the woman I love deserted our marriage, I would be free for the first time in twenty years and so would face the truth that I did not want freedom, that not only would I not feel enlivened by the freedom to do anything I had not done while I was married, but also I would face the recognition that there was nothing I wanted to do. While I was married, I could imagine that if I were not I might make completely different choices concerning everything, but once I was not married, I would face it that I preferred the choices I had made over twenty years or preferred not having made choices at all. It occurred to me that my wife had come to despise me for my *emotional indolence,* as she named it from her new universe, because I had spent years without questioning why they were passing the way they did. I had never thought of my constant need for my wife as shallow—it verified my depth rather than indolence—but if I were shallow, how would I know it?

Though I would come to expect nothing fruitful from the postmortem, nothing would cause me to abandon it, the way my wife was abandoning me, for instance. Even if I deluded myself that the ordeal of the postmortem could elicit a grain of wisdom, once I navigated toward it, I would realize that wisdom was not something I needed. The ordeal would torture me with hope, but I did not believe in hope any more than I believed in hopelessness. The ordeal would torture me the way gray tortures black about the possibility of white, but then it would rescue me, transforming the absence of the woman I love into what I was missing because of it. When my wife and I made love, a triangulation of veins purpled across her forehead, its stem between her eyes, its wings fanning out over her brows in anticipation of a climax that would distort her features further, as if she were in pain, an unspeakable torture rolling her eyes up into her head. Only the whites of her eyes were visible to me during a climax that curled her lip beyond the gumline, where often a particle of food was lodged between her darkest teeth, sometimes a bright fragment of cheese or egg. From deep in my wife's throat, the struggle to ejaculate was a graveled, unearthly cry, until she cradled her breasts between her arms and squeezed her legs so that my ears rang from the pressure. That I would be visited by this scene several times a day, once my wife deserted me, was impossible to fathom, but it was the virtue of the ordeal, its virtue without being its comfort. The torment of my nonexistence would consist of thousands of images that would never again define my reality. My wife smothering my face as she ejaculated, her vast pink thighs deafening me, would haunt my nonexistence during the ordeal, filling days and nights with millions of images informing thousands of insights that no longer could mean anything to anyone. Once my wife has left me, my love will be shared by no one, becoming a state of being love, my essive love, I thought on the terrace. At some point during the ordeal, our love would exist only because of it. It could not continue if I were to see the woman I love, even from a great distance, though the love would be reinforced when, for instance, I viewed our ancient claw-footed bathtub without my wife sinking into it, sending water cascading over the top, ignoring the fact that our bathtub is not the sea, whose depth my wife never displaced, no matter how large she grew. The absence of fresh flowers on our dining table will recall to me the absence of my wife, I thought, so that I do not own a dining table without flowers so much as a dining table whose flowers are missing.

The ordeal of the postmortem would be an effort to articulate my hysteria while still being hysterical. The ordeal would not preclude savage grief or a lifetime of petty complaints against the woman from whom I could never free myself. I foresaw life as inane, banal, accompanied by ridiculous suffering because I had lost the love of the human being I knew best in the history of my life on the planet. The future would become an embarrassment, all the more hideous to bear because of it. It occurred to me that, since I had arrived at a sense of embarrassment, on our terrace, the night of the confession, my wife inside the house must be still more embarrassed at needing to put an end to our marriage, the way a dog is put down, by convincing herself a man other than her husband of twenty years could make her feel happier about life or that, after twenty years of marriage, she had found a man she ought to have married instead of me, or desired to marry because she had been married to me. Even if she believed these things to be true, she must also suspect they were ridiculous. My wife had set in motion a series of causes and effects whose consequences she could not have predicted, but among them had to be a sense of the ridiculous. Even as the entire arc of my life traveled toward inconsolable abjection, I could not lose my sense of the ridiculous about it, which would only add injury to my grief. In a matter of minutes, I had become a shallow, embarrassed husband about to be destroyed by inanity and meanwhile more in love with his wife than ever. I had never loved my wife more than when she was leaving me. To complete the sweep of my shallowness, or the depth of it, I realized that no matter how banal or ridiculous the end of our marriage might become, I needed to salvage my wife's erotic power over me. I could only survive the idiocy of suffering the end of my wife's love for me if I could remain intoxicated by the image of her provocative nudity, no matter how destructive the repetition of it might be. Without her nudity in my mind, from morning until night, the future would be the worst it could be, over and over, the ordeal itself an exercise in banality, if not madness. Even if her nudity did nothing but recall her permanent absence, without it before me day and night, my despair would be the worst the worst could be. My wife's voluptuous nudity had to be preserved, even in her absence, to preserve even my nonexistence. No dark thoughts could interfere with my passion for her nudity, yet there could be no darker thoughts than her nudity. My obsession would redeem tenderness out of misery, even if it was a monstrous tenderness.

Once my wife returned to the terrace, I would explain that I intended to hold in my imagination her constantly nude image, years after she was gone, perhaps decades. I would project her nudity everywhere in our house after she had *débouched* from it, I would tell her. The need I had of her nudity would travel with me wherever I went, in our house and out of it. In fact, after my wife left forever, assuming she did, I would not need to *think* of her nude for her to be nude in front of me. *You do not think of the chair you're sitting in*, I would tell my wife. *I would not be thinking of you*, I could not wait to say, *because I will have no relation to the world other than through you, you and your absence, your nude absence, which rather than costing me my sanity, would be proof of it. It would be the only thing to save of my love for you,* I would explain to my wife, *once the misery overwhelmed every detail of every night and day without you.* The sight of my nude wife standing before me conjured my hands running along her flesh, until I place my arms around her waist, or trace her hips with my fingers, or follow her ribcage down to her hips, then I caress the muscles of her thighs in front and back, and in back I knead the fat of her buttocks as if preparing her for an oven. Though during the ordeal, I would not rely on superfluous detail the way drunks do lampposts; where my wife is concerned, every nuance and blemish, every loaf of new flesh across her belly, will confirm the existence of my nonexistence in the world. In front of her nudity, I used to exist, more often than not, also nude. The future of such images, once she has gone from our house, will reinforce my need to believe in my wife's unhappiness, or even her eventual despair, and that standing nude in front of me for twenty years was the happiest she will have been. If, during the ordeal, I admitted to her new unutterable joy, I would lie down for hours, eyes closed, as if closed eyes prevented me from conjuring my nude wife's new happiness or stopped her throaty voice from documenting her nude happiness without me. It is necessary for me to believe that one day my wife will feel the loss of me as painfully as I will feel the loss of her and that she will discover pleasure is not as pleasurable as she expects and pain more painful than she ever dreamed. This is why I would not remain in contact with my wife after she leaves me, even if she suggested it, suggested that though she loves someone else she wants to know me still, because I am a part of her emotional travels. Because her absence will have ruined my life, I could never see her again. If I so much as saw her from a distance, at a train terminal, for example, I would have to return home, immediately, to lie down, regardless of the fact that I might have been leaving for a month in Venice. As I waited for my wife to return to the terrace, the ordeal had begun to spread like a virus into every corner of my house, every nervure of my mind, drifting around windows and bedposts, gaining familiarity with its new environment, spreading a pandemic of contagion that would mean that at the greengrocer or the *boulangerie* I would see my nude faithless wife squeezing melons and smelling the tails of hot bread; then at the bank the faithless and nude wife would stand in the next file, adding to her wealth while I diminished mine because I could no longer earn a living. My nonexistence would be insupportable, as it should be. *Enough of smelted romance,* I said aloud, on my terrace, in the dark, awaiting my wife's return. The olive grower needed light to hear the sound of my voice, then used darkness to thank me for my silence. However, I was no longer mute.

For twenty years, I had been contaminated by a belief that my wife was essential to surviving whatever was not me. Having attributed to her so much intrinsic value, as soon as I knew she intended to leave, I was condemned to eliciting no meaning whatsoever from the external world. *Once the world is disbanded,* I said while my wife hid her face in shame at my undoing, *nothing else can happen to me. Once you leave,* I said into my wife's laced fingers, *I won't need to speak to anyone again, about anything.* My wife said she had thought I might be relieved at her leaving, which meant that *she* was relieved to be leaving, and leaving would be easier for her if I felt the same. The woman I love ruminated through her fingers that she believed I would enjoy the freedom to be repulsed by everything around me, relieved by the freedom to be odious to others, as if I had spent decades doing so, or wishing I could. Her departure would give me the freedom to despise whatever was not me, including her, she said. Night after night, I replied, for days and for nights, nothing of consequence will happen, nothing will come out of my head, or enter it. While she swallowed wine the way a large bird at a fish pond swallows fish, I explained to my wife that, during the postmortem, I would have to infer her answers to questions I did not yet know, questions I would only be able to form on the landscape of my annihilation, which I had not yet begun to experience, though I was experiencing my visceral preparations for it. I would have to infer all of my wife's responses to the autopsy of our marriage because she had fallen in love and, therefore, harbored no interest in understanding why she had fallen in love. *I love you so much*, I said, *I'll have to uncover horrific flaws in you. I loved you, but you did not me, I, in my chaise, will conclude, across from you, nude, in yours, after you have left me,* I said to my wife, both of us sobbing. *Day after night, and so on,* I said, *I will do the talking for both of us, another feature of my annihilation.* It occurred to me, as I awaited my faithless wife's return to the terrace, that our intimacy must have ended before the adultery began, or the adultery would not have happened, or happened once, but not twice, or at least love would have remained out of the question. Her adultery erased our intimacy, replacing it with contempt on my wife's part, and now a stultifying resentment on mine. It was as if we had never met, or worse, had met, but despised each other. Her departure would not mean oblivion for me, I would tell my wife when she returned to the terrace, not until I died, or she died, but each day I would succumb more to disintegration. Could disintegration be mastered and still disintegrate? If I could be fascinated by the relentlessness of the misery of my nonexistence, would it still be irredeemable loss? Just as waiting for my wife to return meant I was witnessing her absence *before my eyes*, could I consider the end of our marriage another phase of our love? While I could not expect the woman I love to contemplate me and my life as thoroughly as I would contemplate her and hers, it would be impossible for my wife never to remember me once she has left, even if she thought of me with pity, despite being deliriously happy in her new marriage, or even because she was deliriously happy. I would tell my wife that as soon as I realize I will never see her again, everything I want to say and hear will rush into my head, incoherent, incomplete, raving. By the time I could be certain I was asking the important questions, or stating the important statements, my wife would be gone, no longer interested in statements or answers because she had abandoned our space and our time, sighing relief, with a stride into a future of nothing but possibility. The confession would be at an end, like the marriage of twenty years. She would be embarking, no longer disembarking, cementing new friendships, buying clothes, furniture, arranging a new studio, alerting the art media that she had left her husband for another one. Perhaps a new tattoo for the wide expanse of one pink buttock. As for the newest work she would produce, whatever it might be, in whatever media, it would be judged fresh and optimistic, *life affirming*, free of previous constraints, a leap forward, work no one had thought she was going to achieve, a revelation. The artist transformed by love.

At the onset of the ordeal, I would harbor the conviction that my wife must return to me, believing it in order to remain the person I have been for decades. Her permanent absence undid the meaning of our marriage, demeaned our marriage, as I had known it for twenty years, so that everything I understood about it became self-conscious, self-consciously untrue, and I became conscious that everything under the moon about my marriage, and then the moon itself, would be rethought within the ordeal. I was preparing to watch my wife leave, to overhear the tires of an automobile crush the stones outside our door, and then I would see a moonlit starless sky from my terrace that would be a different sky from the sky my wife would see from the window of the automobile, assuming she saw it, or if not, why not, what would she see instead? Within the ordeal of the postmortem, I would gradually become the person to replace the person I had been for the twenty years of our marriage, so that extrapolations about *her* sky versus *my* sky could seem not only meaningful, but essential, defining the depth and breadth of our estrangement. *Don't become desperate*, my wife said, after unhorsing from my lap. *If you become desperate*, she warned, but did not finish the sentence. *If my body doesn't feel the same to you as it used to*, I said, *imagine how yours must feel to me, since it's been mugged. I could feel the difference if I were on the other side of the terrace*, I said to my wife as she buttoned her blouse. *From the earth to the moon, I would sense the difference in your body*, I said to the woman I love. I told her that after she was gone, she could never age in my mind, she would remain stunning, her smell stunning, her skin stunning, so that she must make a point of never letting me see her again, seeing how time will have demolished her. *If I see you in five or ten years*, I said, *I'll be stupefied at what time has done. If our marriage did not end, and I continued living with the body I have adored for decades, the demolition would creep up on me*, I assured her, *minute by minute of minute changes, so that instead of being thunderstruck at the decay time will have wrought, you would remain beautiful to me, still stunning, while to the rest of the world, time will have heaped scorn on you. If I were to glimpse you in the street in ten years or, heaven forbid, at the beach, I would forever see you dragging your carcass out of the sea to a towel under an umbrella where you would need help to sit down and, later, to stand up. As it is, your features will remain as they are tonight, and during the ordeal, when everything else is rethought because of my misery, your luscious body and beauty, your accessible beauty, won't be*, I said to my wife. *Every moment you are not with me, or not returning to me, will be unfathomable, but your body will not. I will fathom it*, I said, *because I will have only the image of your nude body to remind me of myself.* My wife deserted the terrace then, closing her breasts against me by squeezing her fingers across her blouse. I saw the box of Gitanes on the table, saw my glass of wine darker in the darkness. Because of the ordeal, the meaning of our marriage would not be the same for my wife as for me. Before the ordeal, the meaning would have already been different, but differently different before the adultery than after it. For my wife, the marriage was obliterated by a hot blast of love, replacing our hot blast as if it never existed, while for me the marriage remained intact, if inert, even though now, for the purpose of the ordeal, even silence would have implications, and darkness and moonlight appear italicized, in some cases emboldened or bound by quotation ears, to mark the distance between my wife's words, her deeds done, and truths concealed within them. Because my wife was in love and leaving, during much of the confession her words seemed unaccompanied by a sense of our interior life, which led her to paraphrase me when it suited her cause—a further betrayal to which adultery clings, watching the victim eat his own words before the execution. *You've said,* my wife said, *that eventually everyone is miserable because they age, and aging tenderizes us for the slaughter. Eventually, everyone feels sorry for himself out of self-preservation,* my wife said I said. I asked my wife if she was feeling like an old woman; was she acting like a young woman because she felt old and, in fact, was getting old, aging, hefty? *I don't mind you being either,* I said, to cushion the truth. The crossed-out word, unfortunately, is still a word, and during the ordeal, my wife is forever leaving the terrace.

When my consciousness ends, it will end with the last thought concerning my faithless nude wife, though it will likely be an unfinished last thought, last only because there cannot be another, because consciousness, let alone self-consciousness, will be extinguished. It is impossible to anticipate the loss of my consciousness, let alone my self-consciousness, because the world without me in it is inconceivable (unless you happen to be my wife), at least until the moment when not only is it conceivable, it is imminent, then not still imminent, but arrived, then not arrived, then nothing other than nothing. Until then, what used to be consciousness because I shared my life with the woman I love will be self-consciousness because I do not. The consciousness, which was nearly unconsciousness because of our intimacy, will become not only self-consciousness but also the permanent state of anxiety that accompanies it, or what makes the self-consciousness worse, what rubs my nose in it. Even though during the confession my wife released me from the promise to love her forever, which she extracted decades ago and more recently asked me to renew, perhaps because she was afraid she was falling in love with someone else, I could not accept the release because being in love with her was the foremost characteristic of my person, of my humanity. *If you died instead of abandoning me for* the next one, I said to the woman I love, *I would continue to love you, and yet death is final, while sexual betrayal proves that time is fleeting, and when it flees, it flies, like you are about to do. If I continued to love you dead, how could I not continue to love you alive?* She urged me to stop loving her as soon as possible because she could not bear the responsibility. I wanted nothing other than to fly too, to flee to my *next one,* waiting somewhere for me, so that before I abandoned her, I could recount to my stricken wife the torrent of grievances twenty years of marriage had generated in me. My wife said she was deserting the desert of our existence, and I should do the same. My wife felt free, now that she was in love with someone else, to unloose a storm of resentments but as if she were describing a medical condition, as if she were explicating the mental condition of a patient, reciting dispassionately, before lunch on a Saturday, the aberrations accounting for the annihilation of every family member. Because she was in love, her lover's opinion was all she needed to flourish, so now she could clarify how much she had disagreed with me over two decades, since now she was in agreement with *him,* just as *his* desires were the only desires she desired to meet. His needs were hers, his urges her urges, her urges his, and all of their urges urgent.

Even though I am certain she will not, I must believe that my wife will change her mind about leaving me in order to endure the instant I know that she will not change her mind. Only then will my belief be proven false, after the moment when I no longer need to believe. Once I watch my wife, suitcase in hand, walk through our door (vast, wooden, medieval), everything I can remember about our marriage will have been leading to the moment she left, her departure replacing the belief that she would not leave. Nothing will be what it was before she left, just as nothing was what it had been before we married, twenty years earlier. The image of my wife walking away will cement the life of the marriage to the death of it. As she leaves, I will not be able to distinguish the difference between her leaving and her being meant to leave, the event and its being meant to happen. The trauma will be too enormous not to attribute meaning to it larger than the event itself. The trauma will be so momentous that I will need to believe it will also be momentous for my wife because she will know the enormity of it for me. I have to believe in my wife's capacity for empathy, which she cannot confuse with guilt and cannot suppress in favor of twenty years of grievances, which are, after all, coming to an end. Because I will continue to love my wife after she no longer loves me, I will become unlovable, eventually concluding this to have been the case before my wife left me. My wife often said she could not imagine being happier, which I understood to mean that she was happy, instead of which she could have meant that she was unhappy but did not expect the situation to improve, that our marriage was beyond salvation. By the night of her confession, she attributed the collapse of our marriage to falling in love, nothing else, and nothing more, nothing implicating our marriage as the culprit. Even if the ordeal produced an epiphanic moment that could undo my wife's delusion, she would not believe it because the thought process of the ordeal would have outstripped the thought process of anyone not participating in it, let alone someone dripping with passion. Instead, my wife would suggest that my hundreds and thousands of hours studying the death of our marriage should have been devoted to feeding the poor, for instance, or, as in the example of my wife, creating an artistic masterpiece. Even if there were no epiphanic moment and no explanation other than the mystery of the heart to explain my wife's abandonment of me and our marriage, the ordeal would be necessary the way one footfall follows another. The ordeal was simply the next thing that would happen, just as the next thing that would happen to my wife would happen because she was engulfed by an ecstatic belief in perfect bliss, which had swept her away. For her belief to change, time would need to unsweep her. The ordeal would only be of interest to her if her bliss were shattered, and by then she would be embarrassed, or ashamed, or too incurious about the ordeal as my experience of her loss. Waiting for my wife to return to the terrace, presumably to say good-bye, or waiting to hear the quiet click of our door because my wife could not say good-bye before leaving, I was horrified to know that by the time she and I could be civil enough toward each other to have a dispassionate conversation about the collapse of our marriage, the woman I love would have concluded that ending it was the most natural thing in the world, an instance of ebb and flow, our decades together one of the floats in life's rich pageant. The postmortem would resolve nothing, but it would exhaust every nuance of my wife's behavior for years, from the errant unidentifiable pubic hair on our bed sheet to the artwork of bruises and scrapes, like tattoos, that marked the adulteress my wife had become, the nude adulteress who replaced the faithful wife that must have been kidnapped. I could arrive at a recognition, then explain to myself why it was not one. I could explain to my missing wife why she had no hope of constructing a satisfactory life, but she would not be there to be convinced, and if she were, it would be too soon to convince her. The grand themes—dissolute marriage, irretrievable loss, mad love—could only lead to the truth of having assumed too much about each other for too long. I would say to my absent wife, during the postmortem, *if you were unhappy, why not speak up*, to which my departed wife would reply, *if you didn't know I was unhappy, then you must have been unhappy, too.* Or my wife would say that, since I was happy, she hadn't wanted to make me unhappy, until my happiness was nothing compared to her unhappiness. She could say that she hadn't known she was unhappy until she found she was happy in the arms of her lover. Years could pass while the meaningless postmortem defined and occupied my non-existence with heated interrogations that could never take place in the external world. The postmortem that would occupy me for years could not elucidate anything but itself, the way self-consciousness would become one of the themes of *my* self-consciousness.

Paris, summer, sizzling, as the song says, I recalled on the terrace my wife had abandoned. Despite her accusation, I was not a recluse during her travels, not the recluse I would become, beginning with her absence from the terrace the night of the confession. I walked the streets of our town

when my wife traveled, eating lunch somewhere, sometimes dining somewhere with a colleague or strolling into
the woods at the foot of one mountain or another. I was
not a lover of nature, but I enjoyed beauty. I traveled while
the woman I love traveled, even though my career, such as
it was, did not require travel, unlike my wife's. My career
was sedentary, though not a career of the mind, not a life
of higher mathematics, for example, and certainly not an
artistic one. When I traveled, I memorized what had struck
or surprised me to share with my wife, often instances of
human behavior, though just as often attractions, a glock-
enspiel or a ruin. In Paris, in the sizzling summer, I became
ill with flu in a hotel, vomiting, and when not, suffering
bone ache, ear pain, chills, feverish daymares. If my wife
had known, she would have accused me of infecting myself
in order to punish her for traveling again so soon after traveling. If I had wanted to punish her by telling her I was ill,
I could have telephoned, reporting my illness to the desk
clerk, or to the lover pretending to be the desk clerk. Instead
I was eager to tell my wife, when she returned home and we
were reunited, that I had been ill, but I had not telephoned
because I had no desire to punish her for anything. That
would suffice as punishment for believing I wanted to punish her. After a week of flu, I was momentarily eager for the
external world, and though the day was moist with urban
sunshine, I wore a sweater, a woolen scarf, and a sturdy cor-
duroy coat when I greeted the objective universe of which
my wife was so fond. I was not strong; I had not eaten, so
I sat under a shade tree, a nut, and sipped a granita while
I read a newspaper. My stuffy head worsened immediately,
and the warm air made me perspire, as if I still had fever,

unless the warm air had brought the fever back. Being the patient, how could I know? I decided everyone on the street had a secret I might unearth if I watched them long enough. I smoked and watched, but the tribes seemed transparent, unimaginative yet not unhappy with their fates. The clatter of glass and cutlery was giving me a headache. I had come out too soon, I concluded, by now anxious to return to bed and for the first time wondering if I should telephone my wife in case I had contracted a bacterial lung infection, the kind that sweeps the victim away in a matter of days. For an instant, I observed a retired salesman carrying in one hand a leashed miniature dog as he crossed the street, in the other hand his newspaper, which, because the puppy squirmed, slithered from his grip and landed in a puddle created by waiters dumping water against the curb. When the pensioner bent to retrieve the newspaper, he introduced his backside to the street, where a messenger on a bicycle was forced to swerve in order to avoid him. In doing so, the messenger turned toward the front end of a speeding taxi, whose awaiting fare, at the next corner, looked away before the accident, as did I. The retired salesman would leap into eternity, leap into one sentence of the newspaper and, at the instant of his death, meet the eyes of an eye-witness recovering from flu. Before my eyes, the newspaper dropped into the puddle, and the messenger, with amazing dexterity, skirted the pensioner's body, as well as the braking taxi's front grille, before continuing on his bicycle way as if nothing had happened. Nothing whatsoever had happened. I had seen it all. Everything had happened. It took every possible good fortune in the universe for nothing terrible to happen. Nothing happened because everything happened. Remembering the event, the event of the nonevent, as I awaited my missing wife, I wished she had seen what I had seen, months before she needed to confess.

Feverish in the sizzling Parisian summer, I began returning to my hotel, which I could not find; instead I was soon beset by ferocious dog walkers and noisy students discussing late capitalist love in front of store windows and the vast arcades the city is noted for, arcades of glass and human reflections. Young women everywhere had pierced their cheeks but were being kissed in alleys and byways, while the ferocious dog walkers ferociously walked as far from them as possible. Who would kiss lips with pins in them? I wondered. How could I look deep into the eyes of a woman with stapled lids? Did these late capitalist romantics know that as long as they wore protruding metal in their faces, it was impossible to conduct a conversation? Was that why they pierced their faces? I could not have listened to my wife's confession if she had pierced her face. In the middle of a thought riddled with dashes, and despite the heat, I closed my scarf across my throat, mouth, and nose, knowing that I would appear demented to anyone who did not know that I had flu, flu in the sizzling Parisian summer, appearing more demented than people who had pierced their faces. The city simmered with plague, so far as I was concerned, and I wondered where my hotel had been moved during the epidemic. I circled the square, if that is possible, glancing down one narrow street after another, in search of the dangling modifier announcing my hotel, Revenant, a small building whose lift, for instance, could not have accommodated the woman I love and me on our first trip in a lift, twenty years before, when I inhaled her synovial fluid from my fingers for the first time, to say nothing of accommodating the operator with Down syndrome, by now likely dead, who had turned his eyes in horror when he heard my future wife gasp, then choke off the sound of her climax. Perhaps I would have found the hotel more easily had I not been thinking of the past, had I not been cursed by a habit in which the present is always spied on by my memory. I had to sit again and smoke, wiping my face from the heat of the scarf that hid it until the sky clouded and streetlamps spread across rooftops the gentle light that shows cat burglars where to go. Without surrendering myself to Saint-Sulpice by twilight, I lost interest in finding my hotel, instead strolling in search of other people's privacy, hoping to violate it. I had an urgent desire to think I was more like the people on the street than not because it was evening, and I could not bear the prospect of myself for company. I am fortunate that to overcome the dread of being alone, I need only overhear human conversation, and not much of it, and not often, so I stepped into the spaces of couples who were trying, in the wide arc of things, to justify sharing the planet. As soon as I saw a maroon Burberry in front of the booming doors of the cathedral near Vespers, I knew I had seen my wife and realized that I must have seen her earlier without knowing it, which was why I had been spied on by my memory. The retinal image of the maroon Burberry must have triggered the memory of my wife's first orgasm (with me, I mean), waking me from my feverish stupor and the presentiments of doom that accompany feverish stupor. The scream of taxi brakes frightened everyone but failed to draw my wife's attention and drew mine only long enough for me to make certain I was not the target. When I looked back at the cathedral doors, planning to call my wife's name and wave to her to wait for me, the maroon Burberry was disappearing in a gust of wind, a door taller than ten men about to close behind it with a thud. I saw my wife framed by the smoky aura of the cathedral's threshold, where the cold air and incense met in a fog that stopped at the street and where, under the lamps against Magritte's twilit sky, I believed she glimpsed my hand raised in her direction. I might have been wrong, though even so, the woman I love would not have seen her husband but a man who wrapped his face in a wide and flowing woolen scarf, a man wearing a thick jacket with lapels turned up against his neck and ears, waving frantically from the middle of the square. Eager to surprise my wife, I hurried against traffic (more crying brakes), then pushed my way against the great door only to discover worshippers filling every pew, from doors to altar, and ringing the frescoed walls from the candlelit reliquary to the confessionals. As I walked in search of the maroon Burberry, I observed broken-backed war widows kneeling on crippled legs, as if they had been there for years, for years growing through cracks in the floor because they could not move. They shook beaded crosses, praying to the distant altar's narrow tall martyr carved from the marble of quarries in the south, not far from our home, at the moment shuttered and locked against intruders. As usual, the martyr bled at the rib, palms, and feet. I blinked because of the incense, against the dark draft that in my fever chilled me to the bone. I had to sit, I wanted to smoke, and had they served coffee, or a glass of wine, the cathedral would have made a restful spot for conversation or seduction. Had I not been feverish, I would have enjoyed making love to the woman I love on the marble floor. We had never done that, and suddenly it was urgent for me to do it. Once I regained my breath, I looked for the maroon Burberry, listening to my own footfalls on the marble, drawing attention because I walked quickly and forcefully, until the glassy tenor of a priest hiding at the altar shook my teeth. I had no idea why he was celebrating death among a generation of widows grieving husbands whose voices they could no longer recall, forgotten husbands displaced by viscera in jars of other tortured dead men, jars that filled the reliquary next to which I walked still faster in search of my missing wife. Perspiration made a boil at the back of my neck sting, a boil I had not known I had until it opened in the cathedral at Saint-Sulpice, suppurating onto my scarf, the scarf probably the reason for the boil in the first place, unless it was the fever, or a week in wet linens because of the fever. The boil made finding the woman I love urgent, so after missing her from one pew to the next, I pushed open the doors of the confessionals to see if she was confessing, though Vespers was not the time for confession, which would not have deterred my wife if she had wanted to confess, had the religion been hers, had she been religious. The liturgy began in earnest, interrupted by bells ringing from the bell tower, and in my feverish, boil-ridden state, I heard the earsplitting Bach of a Dutch organ above and behind me, then the falsetto of God's voice ringing in my headache. I saw a small door in the transept and dashed for it in hope of recovering my kidnapped wife, or at least to escape the mordant sensation that I was a disturbed character living a symbol-driven existence in a sprawling novel, something Russian. Cathedrals do that even when I am not feverish, though it must have been the fever that selected Russia.

The postmortem ought to be cathartic, I thought on my terrace in the dark, but it would not be, the way most things that ought to be something are something else. Before the ordeal began, I knew it would not serve a human purpose, even though it would bring human thought to bear on unspeakable emotions, as if thinking could comprehend catastrophe, or as if my catastrophe were natural, an earthquake, a monsoon, instead of betrayal. The ordeal would prolong the dissolution of our marriage, tracing the fatal movements of my relations with my wife, forming and re-forming, and revising, over and over, the reality of twenty years, or what I assumed to be reality. The postmortem would be interminable, but no less destructive, as time passed. As time passed, within the eternity of thinking through the collapse of our marriage, there might be moments of nobility, of mercy, even an authentic poignancy that could redeem the destruction, turning it into destiny, or the delusion of destiny. Since my wife's absence would become the object of my obsessive thinking because she loved someone other than me, the ordeal would keep our marriage alive, even when I did not realize she was in my thoughts, even if I believed I had finished thinking of her and that the ordeal was finished. Everything that happens in the ordeal will have already happened, and nothing that happens has not already happened, hundreds of thousands of times before, not to me, but to others. The ordeal has happened elsewhere, to someone else, hundreds of millions of times, but it is no less mortifying to me than if it were happening for the first time in human history. Any question raised by the ordeal would need a lifetime of patient waiting before, at the last minute, it went unanswered, even forgotten, a patient waiting such as I rehearsed on my terrace, in the dark, the night of my wife's confession. Perhaps she wanted me to prepare for the ordeal; perhaps she had spent weeks foreseeing it on my behalf. If the ordeal of the postmortem lasted a lifetime, it might be a way of losing myself in myself, experiencing something reminiscent of memory, but not, so I would not know what happened between my wife and me and what failed to happen. Not knowing the difference, over time, between memory and invention would mean I was not losing myself in myself, but losing myself to myself, or learning that I had already done so, perhaps while waiting for my wife to return to our terrace, perhaps even earlier, perhaps in Paris. Once the ordeal began, if it had not already begun, my nonexistence would be boundless, in time and in space. As impossible as my future seemed, once my wife of twenty years left our house, I would have nothing more to desire, including my wife, and so I would not be bound by desire. Before the end of anything, I realized, people have a lot to say. I had things to say to my wife before she left, if she was leaving, and would have a thousand things more after she was gone. Imagine if, after death, we were allowed to speak. That is what the ordeal is going to be, I realized, millions of words spoken out of one void and into another, and were there an audience, it could only be a force of evil.

Someone had drawn a horizon beyond streets and footbridges, a horizon as distinct as the one I can see from my terrace but below city spires and rooftops—a thread bisecting earth and sea, sea and earth, observing the sun being crushed like an apricot, the purpose of horizons everywhere. The sky blackened, so lamps illuminated Saint-Sulpice from the bistro, where I sat, to the cathedral, now empty and locked and so more severe than ever because it was lit from below. I waited hours, soothing my throat with expensive scotch, then irritating it with Gitanes after Gitanes. I was sitting because my stomach churned whether I walked or sat, and then I was committed to sitting where I sat because of the view. It was a summer's Saturday, the evening of one, when I waited in a bistro across the narrow street where I had glimpsed a woman in a Burberry disappear hours earlier. I had seen the maroon Burberry flee the cathedral, its skirts flying against the breeze, but I convinced myself it was not my wife inside it because the coat was accompanied by a man's sweater, a sweater and a pair of slacks, all of which dashed across the street, joined together by loose limbs as they escaped oncoming traffic and entered the hotel.

The ordeal of the postmortem is going to obliterate the myth of our marriage, I decided as I lit another Gitanes, recalling the night in Paris, then refusing to recall it before recalling it again. At the outset of the ordeal, I would not want to sacrifice the love I have had for my wife, and continue to have, by eviscerating her memory. I would need to preserve our love, including her love for me, which she had forgotten as if she had been struck by a bus and did not remember her name or her life before the accident. Because she is the person I thought I knew, but did not, I am the person responsible for wrong thinking. I am here; she is not; she is somewhere else, I thought on our terrace. None of these simple sentences would crack the cavity of our marriage. To oversee the burial of the last shred of the love I have had for my wife, for twenty years, I would have to embrace oblivion, preserving my love by pulverizing it. The postmortem would be mine alone, outside of the content of our marriage, because I will be the member of the couple to have remained. I remained, she left, and the one doing the leaving has no interest in learning what happened, or why. *My wife is leaving our shared experience,* I whispered to no one. In time, my wife would regret our marriage more than I, despise me more than I would despise her—she would blame me for her unhappiness, or if not unhappiness, then ambivalence. I said aloud on the terrace: *the first morning without being married, the first meal, first sunset, cocktail hour, the end of the first full day since my wife deserted our marriage.* That is only tomorrow, I thought on the terrace, striking a match against the dark.

At the beginning of our marriage, the woman I love would surprise me by revealing at a well-known restaurant, or opera house, or art museum, that inside the maroon Burberry she was nude. If we found a secluded yet public space, my wife would open the coat entirely, nearly allowing it to slide from her shoulders. A park, a parking garage, a busy beach after dinner, even an alley, even browsing the window of a patisserie—in all of these, and more, during the first years of our marriage, my wife teased me with the maroon Burberry, in every instance eventually sliding it along her back to puddle on the floor of our house, the grass of our garden, the front seat of our automobile. Later, it became a ritual of our anniversary—my wife exhibiting her nudity inside the Burberry in public places. Now that I was about to be denied her nudity, whether concealed or not, in public or in private, I interrupted her confession to confess the truth I had withheld for twenty years. *In fact,* I said to her, *I rarely needed to see you nude, though I loved it whenever I did, which was daily, and sometimes all day, because I thought of you as always about to be nude, or just having been nude, or nude, and waiting for me to be nude.* Once she had fallen in love with someone other than me, and once her nudity was meant for him instead of for me, it became the image of her absence, of a lost nude wife of twenty years, the betrayed nudity of the woman I love. The decades of nudity, prior to my wife falling in love with someone else, were swept away by her confession and by the adultery that demanded it. My wife had cooked dinner nude, read books nude, made art nude, sunbathed nude. If there was a mass murder on the television with which we could while away the day, shocked and horrified, my wife would drape herself across me nude, settling in to watch the mayhem. If she lay draped across me for even a few minutes, despite the carnage inside the television I would lift one of her meaty thighs onto my shoulder and lean into her belly with my lips. I had always thought of my wife as provocatively nude, but once the confession began, the nudity meant something other than I had known, the way darkness, and silence, had been changed by the confession. Darkness, silence, nudity—death threats.

How long I sat in Saint-Sulpice no one told me, and I did not ask. I had stared high and to the left so long that my neck ached where the boil's blood had dried, as did my head and stomach, also my teeth. When a pair of doors opened onto a short balcony, lit by a lamp inside a hotel room that appeared to be nothing but a bed, I counted three storeys through the prism of my scotch glass. I observed my wife and her lover, against a light from deep within the room, step into the dark stillness to breathe Paris. I might have seen nothing had I known where to locate my hotel, had I not needed to prove my wife was not the wife I was following, but someone else's wife, a different faithless wife perhaps, whose suspicious husband was sitting nearby with a pistola. Instead, I saw a shirted tall silhouette palm my wife's nude breasts while admiring the spired vastness of the city. He flicked into the sky the dying star of a cigarette they had shared. My wife lifted herself on toes to kiss him, a school-girl's gesture of which she was fond, whether she needed it or not, a way of pretending she was smaller than she was, younger too. After that, I saw her elbow moving back and forth in the shadow of the balcony's iron rail. I could not remember whether the couple went back inside the room first, or if my wife's husband walked away because he had seen what he knew he would see when he saw the maroon Burberry enter the cathedral hours before. I remember that as I walked away, effortlessly rediscovering hotel Revenant a few streets west, I thought of myself as *the husband,* not as I, as in *I am.* The image of my wife's bare breasts in the palms of a stranger (to me), backlit so I saw the lover's silhouette, was to grow into an ineradicable image replacing every image of my wife I had formed over twenty years—not all were erotic images, and those that were erotic were far more erotic than her nude breasts, but none was more erotic than her breasts in another man's hands. The stranger caressed my wife's nipples because they are thick and large, which is why my wife has always enjoyed them bitten, though only where the nipple meets the areola, an areola as wide as a silver dollar, though not silver, but tawny, the color of roe hide. I would come to consider the image of my wife's voluminous breasts, with their wide dark areolas, in the hands of a complete stranger, the most painful moment of my erotic life because afterward, whenever I saw her dressed at home, I saw my wife nude in Paris, and when I saw her nude at home, I saw her nude in her lover's grasp in Paris. Walking back to my hotel, I became the husband in a novelette devoid of martyrs or fevered Russians. No booming voices, no Bach, nothing of an epic scale—instead small, brutish, unsympathetic.

Elsewhere: the locus of my suffering once my wife has left, because she will be where she chooses to be, which she has been thinking of while I have been thinking of here and now, not elsewhere, and not as soon as possible. For the blankness, or blackness, or whiteness of its reality, *elsewhere* will be more palpable than here and now, more palpable than the entire past of our marriage once my wife leaves our house. *After tonight,* I said to my wife from the terrace, *my favorite color is going to be* clear. In the future, I would not be the same person I had been because my wife would not be the same person she had been, which I assumed to be the point of falling in love in the first place. If my wife is elsewhere, where am I? I thought in the dark, on my terrace. *Nowhere,* I replied to no one, already beginning the ordeal by replying to my own questions, replying aloud so as to hear a human voice to replace my wife's, or even someone else's, but not mine. Otherwise, silent thought, as if a neighbor were watching and I did not want to be seen talking to myself or did not want to disturb the olive grower, the watchman wondering what has become of my wife once she has left. Because our house had been ours, once my wife abandoned it, it would instantly become nowhere, nobody's house, nowhere. Just as our house would endure being nowhere, I would suffer becoming nothing in my wife's absence, being the daily and nightly reminder of the perpetual return of nothing new, while my wife's day would be entirely new, and elsewhere, even if something new only waited to happen because she was elsewhere, with someone else. Not so my nonexistence, in which there could be nothing new, over and over, and it would always be nowhere where nothing new happened, in spite of my effort to have nothing new not happen, one of the reasons for the ordeal, even if an unconscious one. The ordeal itself consisted of lightning strikes of memory and storms of detritus, gruesome images of joy and sadness impossible to suppress. Over and over, the mortician breaks open the ribcage of the departed, sloshing aside organs in search of disease that might have been present since birth. After the confession, I would learn that loving my wife was easier in her absence than with her in front of me to contradict my feelings because of her feelings for someone else. The more I expressed my love for her, the more the woman I love regretted having lost her love for me, eventually resenting my love for her, calling it a claustrophobic love. When she loved my love, it was liberating, but when she did not, it was not. Even before she left, I understood that my nonexistence, nowhere, would reduce me to a bundle of symptoms I would never overcome because I could endure them, joining legions of ruined lovers left in the dust of faithless nude other lovers fleeing elsewhere and leaving them nowhere with nothing new. My wife would be the woman I love in my nonexistence because the ordeal of the postmortem will turn loathing into the study of loathing, the futile yearning for my wife into the power of her absence.

The stranger the world seems without the woman I love in it, the more relentlessly it will want to become the realest reality possible, with curves and lines more linear and curvaceous than they were before she left. Without my wife, everything will be more distinct because everything will be shaped by her absence, as if she had been standing between me and everything else for twenty years, blotting out the sun with her large, nude, rapacious body. Darkness will be darker too, but gradually the darker darkness will simply be what I think of when I think of darkness. As with an estranged world becoming reality and the darkest darkness the only darkness, the more I lose of myself as I have known myself, the less I will seem nonexistent, the less surrounded by nothing, the less nowhere, because truth is never nothing. In this way, my wife and I will become more or less than we are, or have been to each other, but still related. Eventually, she will die to me because I will die, unless she dies first, in which case I will die when she dies. Reciting these thoughts to my wife on the evening of the confession, I said that because of her infidelity I realized that for twenty years I had remained closer to her, and truer to her, than I was to myself. *Now what?* I asked my wife. *I know your skin better than my own,* I said, *which means I also know your skin better than you do. Now what?* I asked her. *Just as I used to feel heavier to myself because I was lying on top of you,* I said to my wife, *once you leave me, I will collapse every night into my shadow on the floor.* After two decades, I was suddenly shy about my wife observing the most vulnerable moment of my life, even though she had been present at the previous one, when I knew I wanted to marry her. I asked my wife if she would have been relieved if I had confessed that I, too, loved someone else. *Do you?* she replied with enthusiasm. Because I did not, I realized that my wife must have wished me dead because then the confession would not have been necessary and she would have had the sympathy of our friends and acquaintances instead of their disgust. Once she left, my wife would have little to say about me to anyone, wanting to put the marriage behind her on behalf of the one ahead of her, and so she would patronize me in conversation, offering to others her fulsome praise of me, the praise that victimizes the victim over and over again, and she would avoid our friends so that they could more easily condescend to me. *I know your nostrils better than I know my own*, I said to my wife. I stopped talking, instead thinking of the thinking that would ensue once my wife lifted her suitcases and left me to greet her missing presence. I would observe my wife clothed for the last time as she left with her suitcases. *After that, nothing but nudity, suitcases or none*, I told her. The futility would create in me a self-consciousness shameful enough to demand silence and stillness, which would suggest to anyone in front of our house that no one lives in it. My ordeal will occur in an irreducible privacy, I thought, watching my wife leave the terrace, a privacy as near to burial as possible, though the body still has a pulse.

Once the ordeal begins, I will remember what I had forgotten over twenty years of our marriage because I had no reason to remember it. During the ordeal, I will remember with regret, whether what I remember made me happy or unhappy. I asked my wife if she remembered which painting she was standing before when we first met. For years I did not remember because I did not need to remember, but now that she was leaving, I remembered and wondered if, because she was leaving, she remembered too. Since she was in love with someone other than me, my wife did not remember which city we met in, or which museum, let alone in front of whose painting. The painting, the museum, the city in which they could be found were detached from her memory because she had begun a new one—new life, new mind, new memory. Since I did not want the city, or the museum, or the painting detached from the ordeal I was about to undergo, I did not remind the woman I love that I had observed her from a distance tilting her head, ambivalent about the painting, as if looking at it at an angle might enable her to see it better or to find words for it that would allow it to become a masterpiece. I watched her watching the painting under sunlight riding in through a transom twenty feet high, a sunlight that lightened her blonde hair. My wife's hair is blonde, or used to be. Because she studied the painting, she did not notice her scarf fall to the floor, a silk scarf of yellow and black lozenges, a Mondrian scarf. When my wife asked me to remind her whose painting she was studying when we first met, I refused to say because she was only pretending to be interested and therefore would forget again, asking only because it seemed a safe theme, which it was not. I said that to tell her would violate my privacy. She shrugged, proving me correct, but also making her departure more imminent, beginning to bring an end to our obdurate ending, opening the door onto the universe where whose painting, in which museum, in which city, spoke volumes to me but said nothing to her. I told my wife that if not for the scarf that fell to the floor, we would not have met, not fallen in love, not married, not separated, as we were now doing, and not divorced, as we were about to do. *What scarf?* asked my wife. *Even if the ordeal obliterates every shred of affection between us, nothing will be left in shadows,* I told my wife. I said that one day her nudity would no longer remind me of my love for her, or of her sexuality, or of her sexual betrayal, but that one day, years from now, I would think of her as a faithless nude on a death slab. *Once in a while,* I said to my wife, with tears in my throat, *the nothing I'm going to live will seem like everything.* Her confession had led us to an impasse, where we were irreconcilable, as divorce decrees decree. Which of us entered the impasse first does not matter any more than which painting, by which painter, my future wife was observing when I was struck dumb from a distance by her beauty, then by her intelligent eyes and mouth because I had drawn closer to her to retrieve her scarf. The impasse, our irreconcilable difference, occurred in an instant, similar to the instant in which I was struck dumb in the art museum twenty years earlier. The impasse struck me dumb by making it impossible to look my wife in the eye, her eye not only the window to her heart but also a mirror for me, who was looking for the heart. Looking at each other had become, in an instant, a source of shame, the dreaded sign of the impasse we had reached in which, if she looked at me, I averted my eyes, and she did the same if I did the same. It took a blink of our eyes to realize we were now irreconcilable. Over our decades together, because my wife was an artist, I had come to understand art, until we spoke of the world as composed of the attributes of paintings—suns, skies, water, faces, boots painted or drawn by an artist we admired. At the instant of our irreconcilability, the world as an encyclopedia came to an end. I could not imagine looking at a work of art again without nausea, not even the reproduction of one in a glossy magazine, let alone viewing a rhinoceros as an invention of Albrecht Dürer. I did not yet know which other ways of inhabiting the world were coming to an end, but if my disgust for art was an indication, the nonexistence, nowhere, might have been understated. That was the moment I chose to kiss my wife as fiercely as I had kissed her for the first time. Which painting we had seen twenty years earlier could not matter to anyone who was not me. So, too, the fierce kiss, because we were at an impasse, nowhere, where the irreconcilable go to begin nothing.

Though my wife waited months to confess her faithlessness, I cannot assume that everything she said during those months was a lie. It is inconceivable that my wife would have lied to me about everything because not everything served to conceal her betrayal. The ordeal of the postmortem would distinguish when she lied from when she did not, why one instead of the other, and then, what resulted. I assumed, as I awaited her return to the terrace from the interior of our house, that at least some of the confession would be a lie, though not all of it, because there would be no point to confessing if there were nothing but lies. If she lied during the confession, it would be to spare my feelings, but also to spare herself my feelings about her adultery and, therefore, she would lie to spare herself her feelings about herself, possibly even feelings about the lover for whom she was abandoning me and our marriage of twenty years. Everything my wife had said during the months before her confession, and even during the confession, could have been lies only if my wife were clinically insane, which I would have liked to believe, though I did not, but if everything were a lie, it would be as impossible to know as if everything she said was true, true despite her even being clinically insane. If everything my wife said were true, however, even true only where the confession was concerned, she was certain of her feelings, needs, and intentions, certain of her person, she said, of the direction of her life, which I could not believe because I suffer from doubt and uncertainty on a constant basis, an hourly basis, and assume my wife does too because we have been married twenty years without ever discussing her certitude or my lack of it. I was certain about one thing only, that my wife's behavior toward me during the months before her confession constituted lies of commission, devotions to my personal well-being designed to provide me a sense of security, even a deeper warmth, an indulgence of me that was a sign of matured love. Cooking, baking, bathing me, massaging me, masturbating me—for a time, I feared I had a terminal illness but was not being told. *Under the circumstances,* I told my wife during the confession, *I feel as if I've been fatted up for the slaughter.* My wife said she had not meant it that way, but could understand why, under the circumstances, I could. *I thought I was discovering how much I still loved you,* she admitted, *but instead it was how, not how much, and the conclusion was not good, unless I wanted a roommate. Then too, I felt guilty,* she said, *because the sex with him made me feel so good, I wanted you to feel good too, but I couldn't do for you what he did for me because I love him. In addition to being disgusted by it, I found that having the same sex with you as I was having with him was impossible because I felt that I was betraying him with you, not the other way around. I've felt more unfaithful to him than to you,* my wife confessed. Moments as lurid as this would mean to the ordeal that, on occasion, the autopsy would be rocked by an illustrative find, the history of the marriage reduced to a single image of its deterioration that I would have to live with, look at, and suffer until I lived long enough to suffer less looking at it. Statements my wife made that were meant to explain herself often caused excruciating pain, as if pain rather than explanation had been her motive, or as if they were one and the same. I do not know when my wife lied, but I do not think she lied about the illustrations that caused the most pain, because I think it pained her to recite them. She did not want me to suffer; she wanted me to cease to exist so that her memory of me could cease to exist, so that there could be neither true nor false.

Even as I kissed her, the fierce kiss like our first kiss, opening her mouth with mine and finding her tongue with mine, I discovered not only the impossibility of kindling in her any desire but that, after twenty years of passionate kissing, because she loved someone else, the kiss tasted foul, the act unseemly, more an invasion of privacy than a kiss. No sooner did I kiss my wife than I felt I was assaulting her because she loved someone else. When I mumbled an apology, my wife said that just because she loved someone else she did not feel under assault from my kiss, she did not feel anything at all and understood that I did because I still loved her. I was not a stranger to her, she assured me, I was still her husband, but she understood that she was a stranger to me. *You're the same husband as always,* she said, squeezing my arm, *you didn't betray our marriage; I did.* This was our impasse, at which I had thought I arrived first because my eyes did most of the averting. I realized my wife suffered nothing by looking at me because for her everything had already changed. Instead of looking at what I had lost, I chose to look away, to avert my gaze from my wife's, whose gaze at me for the instant I saw it was one of sadness, perhaps pity, possibly nostalgia, even affection, but not love. She had met the impasse before I did, so that when she averted her eyes, it was because the sight of me evoked tedium, even contempt, which she did not want to reveal. I thought she might be thinking that I had *allowed* her to fall in love with someone else. I had not done anything to prevent it, had not known I needed to do something to prevent it, even if I might have had to ask. When I asked, my wife said that there was not a thing I could have done. I averted my eyes, determined not to look at my wife again. After the kiss opened onto the impasse, we avoided each other's glance, and we did not speak; we did not want to share the same space, the same house, soon enough the same city or country. As soon as the woman I love left the terrace, after the disastrous kiss, and after the disastrous effort to comfort me with her breasts, I began to contemplate the ordeal of the postmortem. The onslaught of ruin, at my wife's imminent departure, was the first indication that nothing of me before I knew her had endured. The moment my wife left the terrace, I felt a stone in the center of my chest. My wife walked away, saying nothing as if she had decided everything. *You're beginning to die,* I said to my wife as she passed a window, glancing in my direction, then fixing her stare as if she were memorizing my face. *Once you leave,* I said into the interior, *we're both dying. Thanks to you, the subject from now on,* I said to my wife somewhere in our house, *is going to be dying and death. How could you not have thought of this?*

Before I began to search the house for the woman I love, or to search for her absence, or to find her gathering her belongings from one room to the next, I walked our house as if it were a museum instead of a small house in the country, though small houses often become museums. On behalf of my wife's memory, I discovered a single heartbroken slipper on the kitchen floor, under the table where she liked to read the news in morning light, though nearby no wife, and in the bathroom, where she also was not, her self-conscious toothbrush turned away from me, looking at itself in the mirror. When I peered into the laundry room from around the corner of the door, I found cringing in the dark an item of lingerie that I did not know existed. The woman I love would not have been caught dead in a bustier, so I had found something she must have worn to please someone other than me because I would not have wanted to see her in lingerie any more than she would have wanted to wear it if I had asked. My wife had been leading another life, which she now wanted to replace ours, one involving bare breasts in public, lingerie, sordid confessions. By sentimentalizing my wife's inanimate possessions, I dreaded the future more than I had moments before. I attempted to console myself that, at this instant of time, I was undergoing my particular trauma, which would be meaningless if it were not happening to me, would be someone else's sad tale were it not happening to me. It was happening to me but not to my wife; something else was happening to my wife—twenty years after having been swept away, my wife was again swept away. Perhaps by betraying me, she had also swept me away again. Why, I asked myself, as I searched for my wife, is there something instead of nothing? I had arrived at philosophy because too many images of my wife's new life surrounded me, including my wife herself. There is something instead of nothing, I thought, as I walked our house in search of her, so that we can begin not wanting it, until in our wisdom we want nothing instead. Searching desperately for the woman I thought my wife had been, I found the door to the universe open like a canyon, like a universe, a high wide door flung wide, as far as the wall, but silently, with stealth, and so not flung, after all, but placed. Beyond the door, in the dark, against the screak of crickets, I heard an engine idling, then footsteps on the stones in front of our house, enough footsteps to prevent me from understanding the muted voices of my wife and someone else. My wife was not alone in front of our house, but I could not overhear a word of the impassioned argument between them, so I retreated to the cellar in search of our steamer trunk, assuming it was the cause of the door drawn wide, but I found it just as I had left it when my wife and I had moved into our house, years before, escaping the chaos of city life, city life's breathlessness. The steamer was where we had planted it and, but for the vermin, happy. I returned to the terrace thinking that I had never left it, so my wife's visitor would be her secret when she returned, and if she did not return, her escape would come as a shock, but a shock without a surprise, so I lit up, sipped dregs, pretending to myself that I expected my wife to return to resume her confession. I decided that my wife's departure was meaningless, meaningless because accidental, or meaningless because inevitable, or that none of what was happening was happening because it could not. Whether my wife remained or departed would not change the changes that her adultery and her confession had wrought in me, in her, and in our marriage. If she returned, I would appear as collected as possible, sipping a cigarette, nursing wine, expecting nothing good, then expecting nothing at all. If she did not return, I would eventually not sit as stiffly as I was sitting. I sat stiffly, as if another person were sitting for me, inhaling oleander, then measuring the sky to see if the moon and the clouds were the same moon and clouds they had been before my wife opened the door to the universe, where her lover resided, and where he was standing in front of my house embracing her.

During the ordeal, the woman I love, and lived with for twenty years, will also be the faithless woman I love, and continue to love, though she has gone. I should take the resemblance between them for granted, not allowing my suffering to cloud the picture of the tall, nude, faithless woman I love with the wife of twenty years, also nude, also tall, but faithful. If I searched for the wife who deserted the marriage within the wife of twenty faithful years who did not desert the marriage, what would it take, and for how long, before I found a fundamental likeness between them? The woman I love was always preparing to leave and knew it, or she became the woman I love preparing to leave. What would it mean for her to be the woman she has been and the woman she has become, both of whom I love and will love, faithful or un-, in fidelity or in infidelity? Since I did not think my wife capable of falling in love with someone else because I have been incapable of doing so, who is the woman I love, the most familiar woman in the world to me, compared to the woman I thought I loved, the woman who will have deserted me for someone else, the most unfamiliar, less familiar than the woman who trims hair inside my nose once a month at the barbershop, or my bank teller, Raquel, whose name I know only because she wears it on a lapel pin above her left breast, with whom I am not familiar at all? By the time of the ordeal, after my wife has left, and I urgently need to explain, if not understand, why she deserted me, I will compare the two women I love, needing to find resemblance, not difference; the difference I know, will know, would know—the difference between presence and absence, themselves the result of love and not love. The failed kiss proved the instant in which the woman I love no longer reminded me of the woman I love, even though she was able to say to me that I still reminded her of her husband but not, therefore, the man with whom she was in love. I was the man with whom she used to be in love. She said that I had not changed, she had changed, so she could say she knew me as well as ever, while I could not say the same of her, or even of myself. The reason I believed that I knew my wife better than I knew myself was that I had observed her for twenty years, and I considered often and at length what I observed of her, all that I gathered to be her authentic self, but I could not observe myself in the same way because I was occupied being myself, as often as not being the husband observing the woman he loves, though not always, not until recently, not incessantly, until the last few months. I believed I knew my wife better than she knew herself because, like me, she was busily being herself, being and becoming herself, busier being and becoming than she could have been if she had been observing herself. What I did not know was that she reserved her being for our marriage; her becoming, the lover. The misreading of my wife's being and becoming ended when I saw her bare breasts in the hands of a stranger on a narrow balcony in Saint-Sulpice. The lovers must have thought they were hidden by leafy limbs of a tall broad elm tree, but the limbs were not so thick, leaves not so dense, trunk not so wide that an interested observer, or disinterested voyeur, could not witness the stranger hold one breast beside the other, as if deciding what he wanted to do with them. As much as I have admired my wife's breasts during our twenty years of marriage, I have admired all of her body, but I never admired her breasts more than I did when I saw them in the hands of a stranger because, for a moment, the startling, bewildering image of betrayal was the fulfilled fantasy my wife and I had shared in our youth, exposing the large beautiful breasts of the woman I love to the objective universe. I did not become obsessed by my wife's body until I saw it in the hands of a stranger, and then I knew her body would define the totality of her, if she left me, and that her breasts would stand for the totality of her body during the ordeal, because the loss of everything my wife had been, and should have continued to be, would be unbearable. The ordeal would consist of thousands of hours of inward speech, in which the events surrounding my wife's departure were repeated and repeated, circled and circled ever more narrowly, on each occasion revealing a new aspect from memory and thought, when what seemed familiar would not have seemed so if I had been a more interested observer of my wife, even though I believed I was always interested in her, never not interested, and sometimes obsessed. My wife could not have been familiar, or at some point, for some reason, while I remained familiar to her, or so she said, we no longer resembled each other enough to recognize that what I assumed to be homogeneity, after twenty years, was hetero-. During the ordeal, thousands of hours of our marriage would be scrutinized, wanton or not, minutely, in order to discover what had been the difference between our authentic passion and what had become *my inner experience.*

This is as good a time as any to tell you, I said to the woman I love. I watched my wife watch me as I entered the bedroom where she lay on her stomach, partially nude, the rest covered by a sheet. I memorized the mole on the back of her left hip, the pegs of her spine, the bowl that one breast formed under her weight. I noticed that the back of my wife's thighs had been marked by the chaise, as if they had been struck by a cane. She looked bruised and sorrowful. After the automobile left and our driveway became still and silent, I found my wife nude, suffering motionless across our bed. When I entered, she draped herself in the bedding, so I stepped out of the doorway and stood in the threshold. *Because I love you*, I said to her, *this is as good a time as any to tell you.* I chose this moment, while my wife lay half nude and suffering to inform her that not once in our marriage had I seen her nude without wanting to have sex immediately, immediately and for hours. *Until now*, I concluded. *Until tonight*, I continued, *until these few seconds of seeing you nude across the bed the way I have always seen you, because until now your nudity was an invitation, meant for me to enjoy.* I did not wait for her to finish my thought. It was time for each of us to finish our own thoughts. I explained to my wife, who had self-consciously wrapped herself in our linens, that my jealousy over her decision to share her body with her lover had increased my desire for her, and that the new lover loving her nudity only made it more valuable to me. *If anything, your infidelity makes me want you more*, I said, *so that there are acts I want to commit with you that you can't imagine I would imagine.* Then I told my wife that, because of those feelings, she was already a distant object to me, with no interior life. She sat up against the pillow, trying to complete my thought, or to navigate its direction. After she lit her cigarette, she smoked, exposing her breasts, thinking my thoughts, suddenly attentive because she had begun to anticipate my words. I retreated to the terrace, telling the woman I love that it was sickening me to talk to her from the doorway while she was exposing herself on the other side of the bedroom. I waggled a finger and vanished from her sight—the only occasion, the night of her confession, that I did the disappearing. During the months since I discovered my wife's adultery, I left her to do the thinking, but I had hinted, speculated, pointed a finger at it many times, hundreds of times, during which she denied everything. With her confession, the dread came to an end, so that no matter how miserable a state awaited me, there would be no doubt. Whatever else existed, once my wife left me, doubt would not. But when, lying across our bed the night of the confession, my wife said she would not leave our marriage, even if she very much wanted to be with someone other than me, I foresaw nothing but doubt, doubt and the despair that nothing but doubt would produce. To be in my wife's presence, I already doubted the next day. When she said she intended to remain married to me, to be married was to doubt, I thought, to doubt without hoping it would one day end, the way I had been expecting first the affair to end, then because it did not, the way I had been expecting the marriage to end. After twenty years of no doubt concerning my wife, a future of doubt felt more to me like certainty, the unhappy certainty of forever doubting my faithless nude wife. I had spent weeks expecting her to leave, but she was remaining, or postponing leaving, even though she was in love with another man and certain she was no longer in love with me, certain that she could not fall in love with me again, could not be swept away by me no matter which sensual, or sexual, or romantic gestures I might perform in the future, a future rife with bitterness and regret, for sacrificing the rest of her life or a future of adultery, the same one or new ones. She lay silent and still, too defeated to lift an arm or move her legs, the same muscular legs that for twenty years had been wrapped around the small of my back, the back of my knees, my neck. But there she lay, nude, reassuring me of her presence by being nude in our bedroom. As for my wife's face, it did not express the ambivalence I had seen twenty years before, when we met in front of a famous painting in a famous museum, but the exhaustion that might result from too much ambivalence for too long about too many subjects. Her face was more a likeness of her face than the face I had seen for twenty years. I had never seen that face, but she must have reserved the expression for moments she knew I could not witness it—dread, exhaustion, defeat, what I saw through the smoky darkness of the room, a pale moonlight from the shutters slicing her skin along thin lines that exposed a crescent of one breast and one creamy buttock. What lay in front of me was a woman's seminude body, but my wife no longer inhabited it.

Before I confessed to the woman I love that months earlier I had seen her bare breasts in Saint-Sulpice, I explained that my self-consciousness would not in the future permit me to think of her without thinking of her as faithless, just as previously I had always thought of her as nude. I would continue to think of her as nude, but from now on she would be the woman I love, faithless and nude, which would undermine thinking about her nudity at all. By now, my wife sat across from me on the terrace so that she could look me in the eye as I spoke. Earlier, she had sat beside me, our bodies separated by the low table holding our cheese, wine, olives, our smokes, so that as she confessed her faithlessness and the love it gave birth to we could look into the sky, not at each other. Now that I had something to say that she wanted to hear, my wife wanted to watch me say it. She sat in the chaise, raising the back of it, as if she intended to read a book. Either she had misunderstood when I left the bedroom for the terrace or had understood perfectly but was completing my thought as if it were her thought, because she sat across from me wearing a pair of white cotton trousers with a rope around the middle and nothing else. My wife sat with her arms behind her head, her hands casually folded across the back of the chaise, so that she exposed her breasts more provocatively than she had in the bedroom, exposing them more than she had exposed them to me in months. With one knee crossing the other and her arms above her head, the woman I love no longer averted her gaze, watching my mouth because I was speaking, watching my eyes because they watched hers. I had said that the maroon Burberry had been more erotic than seeing her breasts exposed under it, so she exhibited them to me now as a memorial to my passion for her, or as a recognition of them as anerotic body parts, like knees or elbows, assuming there are anerotic body parts, though I would not be the one to judge. My wife's breasts were, and always had been, absolutely perfect. The woman I love was, and always had been, absolutely perfect. If she had not been perfect, if her breasts had not been perfect, if her face, her vagina, her belly, her buttocks, her anus had not been perfect, if her humor, intelligence, and talent had not been perfect, I would not have been married to her for decades. Who would do that? There must have been moonlight because bats against it cut the sky like scissors. My wife said she had been surprised by the urge to do something she had never thought of doing. *But our passion,* she said, referring to the infidelity, not the marriage, *created something new that felt like something no one had made before. I didn't realize he had undressed me,* she recalled, *or I him,* she also recalled, *until I saw us together in a mirror of my studio, with my thigh in the crook of his elbow while he shoved his fingers into me. After that,* my wife said, *everything in my life with you was a lie. The more*

I wanted our marriage not to have to end, the more I needed it to end, she said. *Leaving,* she said, *has been the obstacle for as long as I can remember. I won't see him anymore,* she thought, for months and months, meaning me, not her lover. *How does this end?* she had asked herself every hour for months, full of dread, waking to the dread of dread. Because she wanted to go, and I wanted her to stay, we arrived at her unbearable presence, and then mine, which led us to abolish each other, once and for all. My wife's body glistened, lifeless, because she was holding her breath, staring past me, at nothing.

After I informed my wife that I had seen her bare breasts in the palms of a stranger in Saint-Sulpice, her eyes searched for which night, or nights, she might have stood with bare breasts on a balcony in Saint-Sulpice, or elsewhere, for that matter, wherever, and whenever, in Paris, she stood with her breasts bare in public. Wherever my wife's eyes looked, at me, at the sky of bats, at nothing in the near or far distance, they were bewildered and sad at the same time, as if she found my accusation tedious, or belated, which it was, which was why I called it my confession to her. My wife sighed before telling me that, while she had said she would be in Paris for the summer, she had been elsewhere, elsewhere with nameless, often with her breasts bare, bare and in his hands, but not in Paris, she said. *The breasts you saw could not have been mine,* my wife told me with conviction, crossing her arms because I had mistaken other breasts for hers, or so she insisted. *Of course, I don't believe you,* I said. She lowered her arms. *Yes, you do.* My wife's body was the terrain of my truth, her flesh my fate because it had for decades been my constant desire. I could have said to myself, *my fate is sitting across from me for the last time.* I could not imagine wanting to see every day and every night any face on earth other than the face of the woman I love. In her absence, I wanted to say, but did not, I would make myself odious, if I was not already, so that I would never run the risk of loving, or being loved. If the exposed breasts I saw in Saint-Sulpice did not belong to my wife, and I admitted no such possibility, then they were even more nuanced for me than when she concealed them inside the maroon Burberry. In losing my wife, I collected what I could still love about her without being reminded that she had fallen out of love with me and into love with someone else. That is why people who leave other people eventually are divided into parts, becoming human remains discovered at the scene of a crime. My wife had told the new lover that she could not leave her marriage when he had arrived to liberate her from it an hour earlier. I could not imagine life without her, so I began to experience the unimaginable by choosing to end our marriage on the spot. I asked my wife to vanish as if she were an odor. I asked to divorce as soon as the sun rose, if it was possible. As a joke, I volunteered to pack and leave. I told my wife that since I had always thought her beautiful, the loss of her beauty was going to be sublime. She would not experience the sublime as I would, I told her, she would need thunder, lightning, failure. I would undergo the unspeakable sensations of dread and formlessness and would not be thinking about her after she was gone so much as thinking of the thought of her. I would be trapped in my thought of her, thinking I was thinking of her, but I would always be thinking of losing her. I would experience an even more powerful emotion than my love for her because my love would no longer have my wife as its object. It would be absolute love, absolutely empty of a person. *How does it make you feel,* I asked my wife as she left the terrace, *how does it feel to know that you're already starting to forget you ever knew me?*

Beaune Margaux, wheel of cheese, olives, pits of olives, Gitanes, Gitanes stubs, the mark of her lips on the rim of her wineglass—the debris my wife was leaving in her wake. For the remainder of the night on which our twenty years of marriage ended, I wandered the house wondering what she had left behind and what she had taken in two suitcases, what therefore she valued and what not, but I did so hearing my wife's voice inside my head, naming objects as I found them, or failed to. At some point, I heard an engine idle outside my house, the familiar scrunch of stones I had heard hours before, then two doors closing instead of one, as I had heard hours before, and the engine went away, slowly, until I could not hear it. When I was not wandering from room to room or standing with my eyes and ears closed, I sat on the terrace waiting for my wife to return because there were thousands of things to be said, and I had already changed my mind about ending our life together. I spent the night on the terrace certain I was hearing the door to our house open and close, the way I used to believe it was opening and closing when the woman I love traveled longer than I liked. Only at the first light of day did I go to the door of our house to be certain my wife was not sitting in front of it on her suitcases, and then, once back inside, I lifted the receiver to make certain our telephone was in order. I saw the set of house keys she had left behind on a window ledge and realized I had begun my life without the woman I love. However she might have pleased me, whichever forms the pleasure of knowing her had taken, or the memories of my own life that placed her in front of me—all these were inane and meaningless as the purity of her being gone forever washed across me. I sank into the sensation of her loss until I felt my wife's contempt because I asked myself what she was doing that minute, then the next minute, and the next, filling days and nights with futility, awaiting the ring of the cowbell, or the telephone, or the postman, able to sleep only if I concluded that my wife, having given and received one or two orgasms, in one or two orifices, was herself asleep. If she was sexually spent, I was emotionally exhausted. If I could spend my days and nights nurturing her disgust of my weakness and her relief at no longer having to see or hear me, no longer having to witness my thought and behavior, then I could survive our permanent separation by refusing to give in to them, her relief and disgust. She had said, with her voluminous breasts exposed on the terrace, *you* don't need me anymore, a way of saying that *she* didn't need *me*. What had been for decades *you and I* had become *he and I,* italicizing the fact that we must have always been separate and alone, that in spoons at night in bed, we may as well have been thousands of miles apart, planets apart, different species on planets apart, because human beings delude themselves that someone will love and understand them until they die. First, *you and I* will understand each other until we die, then *he and I* will do it.

After I realized that my wife would not return to me, her absence seemed impossible. Even if my thinking had been limited to her loss, the loss was the theme of my existence. I knew no subject more completely than my wife, despite the unfortunate truth that I did not know her as well as I had thought, so I knew the loss of her better than anything else I knew about her. While I had no one to share my thinking with, I thought, without limit, of my impossibilities, of my unlimited impossibilities, including despising my marriage as much as its postmortem. Pleasant memories of my attraction to my wife repelled me, their images vanquishing my desire for her, and when I could not suppress my sexual desire, I enjoyed, without relief, the absence of her flesh pressing against mine, flooding over me the way her thick body used to when we wrestled to a mutual climax. My suffering could become ecstatic, nearly blissful, when I tried to comprehend why the woman I love deserted me, then why I could not stop thinking about it for more than a minute. If I forgot to think or to suffer because of it, I would startle myself, returning in an instant to my misery, as if to think anything else were heresy. I was captivated by the magnitude of my loss, so I identified my wife's absence with ineradicable despair. Without her, I could not be anything other than the result of her absence, but with her, for two decades, I could not have been anything other than the husband waiting for his wife to leave. I saw my wife nude everywhere I went, sometimes even nude inside the maroon Burberry, sometimes simply nude on the street, when I went into the street, which was rarely. Her public nudity reminded me of her faithlessness, so eventually any nudity I might glimpse, anywhere, reminded me of it. My obsession enabled me to love my wife without the nuisance of familiarity—our quotidian life could not erode my passion. My passion had no obstacle, including my wife, and no living person within miles who could dampen my ardor, particularly after I posted my letter of resignation and was no longer expected anywhere, by anybody, ever. I was relieved of looking anyone in the eye again. Though achieving a condition where my wife's absence overwhelmed any power her presence had ever had, I knew I had been abandoned and abused. My outrage, and its opposite, were all that remained of the man who loved the woman I love. I loved the thought of her absence because otherwise I would have had to acknowledge her ongoing humanity, which was inconceivable. When she left me, she ceased to exist as the person I had known for twenty years because the person I had known would not have left me. The woman I love was beautiful because I loved her, sad even though I loved her, then gone because I loved her after she no longer loved me. If my wife were the same person now that she had always been, then she must have been the embodiment of my needs, the person I needed her to be until it became clear, only to her, because of her new lover's needs, that she was not. Once she was gone forever, the woman I love became the fate of my needs that were now not going to be met, ever. Continuous images of my wife transformed her into a delirium of my unmet desires, unattainable fulfillments, as if, because our life together had ended, it had never taken place. I had not been fulfilled by our marriage, but I had accepted that neither is anyone else by theirs. Suffering the unattainable nature of my wife, I would understand her to occupy my inevitably failed past, my decades of delusion; in the delirium of unmet desires, I defined my wife as an inconceivable woman, not only absent, but also formless, her reason for leaving therefore a search for form. For the decades we were together, I was saturated by my wife, bathing in her presence. Now that she was gone, her absence saturated me until I concluded that I no longer needed her in the flesh. The more I could not forget her, the more certain I was I did not need to see her or to speak to her again.

I suffered only my obsession with her absence. At first, my constant thinking about my lost wife would make everything that was not her, or not about her, outrageous. I could fly into a rage on any street corner, in the middle of any shop. In fact, shopping became impossible, for days at a time, because I would fly into a rage wherever I was, terrifying the world by storming off, abandoning my unbought goods in a heap on the floor. Gradually, instead of outrageous, I found everything that did not address my wife irrelevant, then later I found everything that interfered with my obsession irrelevant. Over time, the obsession sustained itself, which, I suspect, is the definition of obsession. It would have survived an earthquake, perhaps even the end of the world that I was expecting every day. I would no longer yearn for my lost wife because she was no longer the person I had mistaken her to be. Her effect on me became the subject of my thinking, until I would recognize my wife in bouts of nauseating vertigo or pains high inside my colon or in the breathlessness of darkest night. The ordeal became thoughtless, until I was irreducibly and ineluctably myself and unable to conceive of being any other way.

A sultry haze consoled me for the futility of all endeavor. I refilled my cup of coffee while looking at the sky, since my coffee, because of the hot cream, resembled it. I could see from the treetops a breezy morning, breezy as well as hazy. At some point, if the breeze continued, the haze would disappear. I stubbed my Gitanes against the stone wall of the house, a habit I had recently acquired, then immediately lit another Gitanes, another habit. If there had been a witness to my acquired habits, she would have discouraged all of them. I eyed my wife's empty chaise with suspicion, as if it wanted to move next to mine. I cradled my coffee and box of Gitanes and nearly made it to my missing wife's empty chaise, intending to take it over once and for all by sitting in it, making it mine instead of hers, when I had an uncontrollable urge to look over the terrace wall onto the stone path below. I gave in to the urge, a waste of time, but one that straightened my thinking, so I adjusted my wife's empty chaise until it faced mine across the terrace, angling the back as it had been angled by the woman I love when she last occupied it, when it looked as if she might start to read a book by moonlight instead of listen to my confession. With Gitanes and coffee at my side, I returned to my chaise and stretched out in it before looking over at my wife's chaise. *That's the way she was*, I said to myself. *That's the way you are*, I said to my absent wife, *delivering bombshells, then leaving the room*. She had worn only cotton trousers ending not at the ankle but at the calf, loose at the calf, unlike Capri pants, which are tight at the calf. The night on which I last saw my wife across from me on her chaise angled for moonlight, she wore only a pair of white clamdiggers, despite her thick ankles. Moonlight poured over her shoulders. She said that I was obsessed by the past, even the recent past, judging it as more meaningful than the present, or if not more meaningful, more useful in explaining disappointment. My wife considered my memory hostile and its conclusions pitiless. I assumed she was saying these things in order to make deserting me seem a dispassionate act. She said, with bitterness, that I used regret for the past to sabotage the present. She had never thought of herself as disloyal, she said with anger, until she became disloyal, then became dishonest because of it, then cunning, a word she would never have used about herself until now.

Once she had become all these things, she knew she was in love. As soon as my wife has left me, I decided while she was talking, thinking to myself instead of listening, I will eliminate every sign of her existence, even while whispering in my head *we'll never be finished.* Later, I was comforted when I no longer walked into a room wondering what the room was doing without my wife in it. When I found the shape of her head in a bed pillow, I left it for weeks, until thoughtlessly I fluffed it, as if her head had never existed. I studied the dove gray sky the breeze was making of the haze, noting it was the dove gray of a winter noon, even though it was neither noon nor winter. It was after winter and nowhere near noon. By the time I returned my eyes to my wife's chaise, her image was in it, bare-breasted in white clamdiggers, her lips pursed to enumerate my flaws, one brow tilted as if she knew something I did not. Her image evoked the memory I would carry into my grave. My wife was seated across from me, as she had sat across from me on the night she and I confessed to each other, but now she sat because I had suppressed the moonlight pouring over her shoulders and had concealed, inside my dungeon of memories, that my wife's nipples had stiffened. She had smiled with affection and gratitude, hoping to reflect the intimacy of twenty years together, but it was because the twenty years had come to an end. She did not know, or did not care, that the cool breeze, or my confession to her, had stiffened her nipples. I wanted to ask my wife if she had been aware, while listening to my confession about seeing her in Saint-Sulpice, that her nipples had grown erect, erect but soft, as thick as my thumbs. Why? Another signal recognition out of the blue of my memory, one among thousands, born from obsession, creating obsession, reminding me that my wife and her body existed differently from the way they had existed for decades. I sipped the haze of my coffee, completely exhausted because of my absent wife's inexplicably erect nipples. I crushed my Gitanes, lit another, then heard footsteps on the stones below, just as I had thought I heard them when I first noticed the haze and then the breeze that cleared the haze away. I had not heard a sound since the night my wife left, other than those of my own making. I was frightened to look, in case the intruder was not my wife, but I was more eager than frightened in case she was home.

When I observed my wife across twenty years, I inferred that she was happy, or if not happy, content, though more often than not she said she was happy, sometimes as happy as she could be. *I can't imagine being happier,* my wife often said if I asked her if she was happy. After she left, I would recall the expression on my wife's face, a confident satisfaction that accompanied her attempt to observe me when she did not think I was observing her, just before she would volunteer an exclamation of love for me and the happiness it brought her. What if what I had taken to be a thoughtful, warm expression was a sad one instead? Was my wife reassuring me of her love or trying to convince herself of it or forcing herself to remain in our marriage by committing herself to words she knew I would believe? I would not have known she was sad unless my wife had said she was sad, and since she did not, I assumed hers was a contented expression. I could have mistaken decades of melancholy for peace of mind, and my wife could have mistaken monotony for intimacy, tedium for security. The ordeal would contain thousands of recognitions drawn from everything I once thought superficial or trivial, assuming greater and greater significance until it was profound and permanent, permanently profound—a sign of destruction. I asked my wife if she had felt self-conscious being nude in front of me once she had fallen in love with someone else. She replied that she had avoided it, except when avoiding it would have risked revealing her affair, and then she did not feel self-conscious so much as remote, as if her body did not exist, or she was wearing someone else's. When she thought of her nudity, she was nude with her lover, not with me, she said. I asked her if she had been thinking of her lover when, the week before her confession, I found her masturbating in the bathtub. The water had sounded so turbulent from the kitchen, where I stirred our salad, that I feared my wife was drowning. Too late, and pointless, pointless without being untrue, the ordeal would eventually be more meaningful than our marriage of twenty years, becoming the most mean-ingful experience of my life because it contained everything and achieved nothing. During our twenty years of marriage, I never considered the meaning of anything, taking meaning for granted, the way I took interest in my wife for granted. There was meaning because I was interested. Once the ordeal began, I would only be interested in everything I associated with my failed marriage, whatever pointed to our ruin, to our annihilation as husband and wife, including gratuitous images of sexual excess, then betrayal. My memory wandered the smoking deathscape of a glandular science fiction, the horror of my wife's sexual pleasure. I realized that, when she left me, my wife had escaped my thoughts and opinions, my view of the world, divorcing not only me and my thoughts but also how I arrived at them, fleeing the restlessness that had finally found a subject worthy of attention—the fiasco of our marriage. I wanted the ordeal to discern how intimacy had become shame and embarrassment, emotions I had never attached to the woman I love and could not have conceived would be the last emotions I felt in her presence, and she in mine. Our detachment from each other was all we shared.

His appearance does not matter because it was someone else's reality, and so I resented the unknotted necktie, the leather bombardier, the sneakers on his feet. I would have resented tee shirt and jeans or a tuxedo, just as much or as little. He studied the rooms of our house, drank a glass of water from the tap, as if he had done so before, which was impossible. *My wife left me for a man with a lock of hair across his eyes,* I said more to myself than to him, but said nonetheless, while I watched him finger it aside, then finger it aside again. My wife's lover was the first person to have entered our house since she left me for him. He was searching for her, he said, lipping one of my Gitanes into the corner of his mouth, so that when he spoke I had to listen carefully to understand him. *She shaved her head,* he said with disbelief, as if he had been insulted and expected me to share the insult. *You know her better than I do,* he said. *Where would she go?* I replied that I did not know my wife better than he did because she had left me for him. On the terrace, where I did not tell him his body stank, we had one neat scotch each, standing in front of the olive grove and, beyond it, the sea, where a storm in the distance would have capsized small vessels. Nameless said he could not bear to live without my wife because they had waited years to be together, then he discussed their life in detail in order to find her departure incomprehensible. I was not offended by his sexual candor, but I did not return it, thinking instead of the final years of our marriage, several of them. I sent him away in a driving rain, his return to Paris urgent because, wherever she was, he concluded, he was certain she would not have come home. My spirit should have been lifted, but it was not, and I should have begun wondering where my wife had gone, wondering if she wanted me to find her now that she had shaved her head. My spirit was not lifted because now that my wife had abandoned her tempestuous affair, she was embarking on a life that would be more detached from mine than when she was only in love with someone else. While she was in love with the lover she had deserted me for, I was the deserted husband. Now that she had deserted the lover, as well as me, I was receding further from her life, and she from mine. Since she had deserted him, the woman I love had begun storing memories I could not imagine. No matter how badly I thought I would feel if my wife ever left me, once I ended our marriage the reality was worse, but not as bad as the reality that my wife had disappeared completely by ending the affair. She had disappeared without informing me that she would. In the future, I might read about her in a newspaper, assuming I began to read newspapers again, which we had done together for twenty years, so it was too soon to say. I no longer faced the possibility of further human disillusionment, nor could I be disenchanted. By leaving her lover, my wife left me again. I returned to the terrace after the spurned lover left, reclined in the chaise, my chaise, watching and then feeling the spray of spring rain. The rain's monotony calmed me enough to settle in with what remained of the scotch and Gitanes; the glass of scotch I held to the light within the rain, the Gitanes I held beside the scotch before I fired it up, comforted by the monotony of the smoke. My wife—nude, bald, oiled for the sun—smoked across from me.

Whenever I saw her face, I never wondered what she was thinking. When I saw her, I saw the woman I love who was my wife, but now she was the woman I love who was not my wife. She will always be *not my wife,* but the woman I love. An explanation for my wife's years of infidelity should have been written across her face, should have been discernible for years, not only before she left, but also before she took a lover, and before that there should have been signals that she was going to destroy our marriage someday, even as soon as possible. I advanced from experience to experience, throughout our marriage, seeking instances in which I overlooked or suppressed a warning, or in which my wife suppressed or overlooked a warning, something that did not have to reveal an intention on her part but which could have suggested a resolve, even a hidden resolve, to dissolve our marriage. Even if my wife had feigned her love for me, if part of her resolve to leave our marriage was to feign loving me until she could not feign it anymore, or until she found someone with whom she could fall in love, there must have been thoughts, unformed ideas, there must have been words in her head, on the tip of her tongue, dreams in the night. *You can pretend to be asleep,* I had said to my wife the last time she lay seminude across our bed, *but you cannot pretend to be awake.* My wife was truthful after she had spent years being untruthful, telling the truth when it could injure no one but me, though she would not have thought that to be the case, but only when she and the lover concluded that they needed to live together because they loved each other so much did my wife tell the truth, when telling the truth could do them no harm, and then she lied not only to me, but to her lover, lying to him because she was lying to herself, or not.

After I told my wife that I had seen her bare-breasted on a balcony in Saint-Sulpice, she replied that not only had she never been nude in public in Saint-Sulpice, but also that she did not believe I saw anyone's bare breasts when I was suffering flu the previous summer, if I was suffering flu, if I was in Paris. Mine was a desperate effort to extract a confession from her, she said, accusing her falsely in order to extract a different unpleasant truth. I told my wife that if in an impossible future we were to meet in the street, she was to pass without a glance. If I saw her leaning into a taxi, in her maroon Burberry, for instance, I would instantly see her nude, leaning over to expose her nudity to the world. *One day you're visiting a zoo*, I said to my wife as she was closing a suitcase, *the next day you're in the jungle.* The ordeal of the death of my marriage to the woman I love cannot spare me morbid thoughts, but I continue to think of her loss because I cannot know the next thought I am going to think. Only today, I discovered the maroon Burberry hanging on a hook behind a door in the cellar. It looked like a suicide.

1989–2009